A Candlelight Ecstasy Romance®

"THIS IS THE FIRST TIME MY FATHER'S EVER TAGGED ALONG ON A DATE," CHARLA MUTTERED.

Kirk grimaced with wry amusement. "He invited himself. It's a little awkward telling your father to go jump in the lake."

"Feeling outmaneuvered by the chaperon?"

His hand rested on her hips as they joined the other couples on the dance floor. "It's too early to give in yet. And your father's making it hard not to accept the challenge."

"Am I being put on the alert?"

"It might be wise, unless you're ready to concede defeat."

She laughed. "Kirk, the war has just begun. That trumpet you hear is really the bugle calling the reserves to arms."

"Speaking of arms, I like the way yours feel around me . . ."

CANDLELIGHT ECSTASY CLASSIC ROMANCES

CANDLELIGHT ECSTASY ROMANCES®

THE BEST REVENGE

Edith Delatush

A CANDLELIGHT ECSTASY ROMANCE®

Published by
Dell Publishing Co., Inc.
1 Dag Hammarskjold Plaza
New York, New York 10017

Dell ® TM 681510, Dell Publishing Co., Inc.

Candlelight Ecstasy Romance®, 1,203,540, is a registered trademark of Dell Publishing Co., Inc., New York, New York.

ISBN: 0-440-10483-1

Printed in the United States of America

June 1987

10 9 8 7 6 5 4 3 2 1

WFH

To Our Readers:

We have been delighted with your enthusiastic response to Candlelight Ecstasy Romances®, and we thank you for the interest you have shown in this exciting series.

In the upcoming months we will continue to present the distinctive sensuous love stories you have come to expect only from Ecstasy. We look forward to bringing you many more books from your favorite authors and also the very finest work from new authors of contemporary romantic fiction.

As always, we are striving to present the unique, absorbing love stories that you enjoy most—books that are more than ordinary romance. Your suggestions and comments are always welcome. Please write to us at the address below.

Sincerely,

The Editors
Candlelight Romances
1 Dag Hammarskjold Plaza
New York, New York 10017

THE BEST REVENGE

PROLOGUE

Charles Treemont set the golf ball on the tee, lined it up with his number-three wood, and hit it solidly. The ball soared straight and true down the fairway. Then, perversely, it hooked and dropped in the tall grass lining the side.

"Damn!" he muttered, and stomped away so his partner could tee off.

Tyson Webster smiled indulgently at his old friend. "I don't know why you let it get to you. You know that's where it always lands."

Charles glowered. "I was doing fine until Baswell insisted on boring us with those pictures of his grandson. It ruined my concentration."

They had caught up with the party Baswell was playing with, and until he had moved on, the proud grandfather had cornered them with pictures of his new pride and joy.

"You'd think he was the one to invent grandchildren," Tyson agreed. He swung and watched with satisfaction when the ball landed in the middle of the fairway. True, it hadn't gone as far as Charles's ball had, but at least it was an easy play.

They climbed in their golf cart and drove on. When the balls fell in the cups, they matched out with a four on their scorecards. They had played together since they were teens, and their final scores never varied more than five points from each other.

"At least he *has* a grandchild," Charles admitted grudgingly fifteen minutes later after they had teed off at the sixteenth hole.

Tyson had no trouble picking up on the conversation. Being lifelong friends, their thoughts often took the same direction. "We would, too, if those stubborn children of ours were married."

"Charla practically froze the tail off the last man I brought to the house," Charles grumbled as he selected a wedge to get his ball out of the sand trap. "I don't know what to do with her. You have to admit I produced a darned good-looking daughter. I was certain she'd never make it through college single, and here she is twenty-eight and not even engaged. Not that she hasn't had plenty of offers," he added hurriedly.

Tyson didn't need reminding. He'd commiserated with his friend through all the lost opportunities. "You can say the same about Kirk. He's thirty-two and has built his business to the point where it practically runs itself. Maybe if he wasn't so handsome he wouldn't have so much to choose from and would find someone to settle down with. Of course, with us as role models, we can't exactly blame him."

The two men exchanged grins hinting at shared memories of those long-ago carefree days. They had cut a mighty swath through the delectable ladies abounding during their experimental youth.

"Still, we didn't get married until we hit thirty-five," Charles reminded him.

"And we were so immersed in our life-style that we almost missed recognizing them when we found them."

Eyes grew soft with memories of the women they had been fortunate enough to talk into marrying them. After months of desolation, however, they'd come to accept that Greta and Sara wouldn't be with them to enjoy their so-called golden years.

Charles swung and the ball curved upward in a spray of

10

sand. He gave a grunt of pleasure when it landed a short putt from the hole. "We're not getting any younger, Tyson. If those children of ours don't get going, we'll be too old to enjoy our grandchildren."

"I've given up pushing Kirk. He said if I don't get off his back, he wouldn't come home anymore."

"I'm hearing the same grumbles from Charla. She threatens to move out. I guess I'm selfish. She's too good at running the house, so I guess I have to back off."

"With the headaches they're giving us, those two stubborn ones deserve each other."

Charles jerked in the middle of his putt, topping the ball. He straightened to stare at his partner. "What did you say?"

"Those two stubborn ones deserve—" Tyson's eyes brightened as he tuned in on what had struck his friend. "Are you thinking what I'm thinking?"

Matching broad grins spread across their faces. "Where have our brains been? Those kids practically grew up together until Kirk went to college." Their grins grew wider. "If I remember, where one was we could always find the other." Charles slapped Tyson exuberantly on the back. "By golly, I think we've got it!"

"It's going to be tricky getting them together."

"Has that ever stopped us before?"

"They've become gun-shy."

"Then we'll have to plan this carefully."

Tyson rubbed his hands together gleefully. This was like old times. "What we need is a war plan."

Golf sticks were thrust hurriedly into the bags, and they drove to the clubhouse, bypassing the rest of the holes. This demanded careful coordinating.

The afternoon was spent with two white heads bent together as they developed their attack with Mephistophelian glee.

11

CHAPTER ONE

The sun was halfway down on its glide to the west and unrelentingly hot. The Jaguar turned from the highway onto a secondary road, and Kirk Webster reached for his dark glasses as the sudden glare reflected from the hood. He was tired and angry and wondered what the gods had against him. He'd cleared his calendar so carefully with the hope that this time his well-earned vacation would remain uninterrupted.

New Orleans had had a lot to offer, and his trip had started out well. After two days a certain dark-eyed beauty had shown all the signs of being willing to make the vacation perfect. But then the call had come.

So now he was on the road to Santa Fe, the last place he wanted to be.

He frowned, reviewing the phone call from his father two days before.

As usual, Tyson wasted no time getting to the reason for the call. "I'm sorry to be doing this to you, Kirk. I know you've been working hard and need this vacation, but Charles is in trouble."

"Treemont?" Kirk had just finished showering and was toweling himself. His attention was focused out the window and on the hotel pool two stories below. It was already draped with an assortment of beauties, and if he wasn't mistaken, one of them was the delectable lady who had caught his interest.

13

"Of course it's Treemont." His father's annoyance at his obtuseness brought his attention back to the conversation. "This is the fourth time one of the machine parts his company makes was rejected by the government. Somehow it slipped past his inspectors."

"Then he better reevaluate their inspection system."

"Believe me, he has. It's tight and it's thorough."

"Obviously not, if defective parts got through." His gaze drifted back to the pool.

"Charles is thinking of sabotage."

That got Kirk's full attention. His success quotient in solving that type of problem was what had built the reputation of his company, KW Investigators. After several years serving the FBI, it had proved less than satisfying. He had discovered that he wasn't happy working under strictures. But he was thankful for the top training they'd given him. "I thought Charles no longer headed up his company?"

"He's still chairman of the board. Look, Kirk, I checked this out before calling. He's been warned. You know how the government can be. One more slipup and they'll cancel the contract. With the way the economy is, losing it could drive his company under. He's got problems and needs you. I told him you would do this for him."

Kirk heard the quiet pleading behind the words. The two old codgers had been buddies since childhood. If Charles's company went down, his father would suffer along with his friend.

Since going to college, he had seen Charles Treemont on infrequent occasions. Before that, when Greta Treemont and Kirk's mother Sara were alive, the families had been close. In fact, most holidays and vacations had been spent together. He guessed he owed one to Charles for the many happy childhood memories.

He heaved a sigh and turned his back to the window. Good-bye sweet Creole lady of the inviting dark eyes.

And so here he was on the second day of his trip to

Santa Fe. He'd driven the day before until exhaustion had made him settle for a small hotel in Sonora, Texas. It would have made more sense to fly in, but then he would have had to hunt for a place to leave his Jaguar in New Orleans. Besides, he had no idea how long this would take.

He reached for the pack of cigarettes and muttered in annoyance when he realized it was empty. It was just as well. He'd been smoking too much lately, a sure sign that the pressure of work was getting to him.

Knowing it well, he barely noticed the barren landscape. This was arid territory where the red earth struggled to support meager stands of shrubby sagebrush and yucca.

He was tired and fought the hypnotism of the straight roads that seemed to disappear into infinity. Even the stark beauty of the buttes failed to appeal to him.

His long tan finger pressed the window button, and the glass slid silently down. The buffeting wind should help keep him awake, he thought. It felt good ruffling through his white hair.

Kirk glanced in the rearview mirror. His hand pushed back the thick pelt as he grimaced over memories. His black hair had turned white while he was still in college. In those hell-for-leather days, he'd been quick to take advantage of the interest it produced from women. The contrast with his black eyebrows shielding pewter gray eyes brought all the attention he could handle.

He'd mellowed since those days. He loved his work since leaving the FBI, and building his company to its present position took most of his time. Which was one reason he had looked forward to his vacation.

A glance at the mileage gauge alerted him that the approach to Treemont's house was near. He would have preferred the freedom offered by staying in a hotel, but Santa Fe was having one of its big powwows that brought together all the neighboring Indian nations. The city was booked solid with tourists crowding in to inspect the various tribes and their rituals.

15

It had been years since he'd been at the Treemont's, and the entrance to the driveway came on him suddenly. Although he'd been watching for it, the small sign almost escaped his notice. The tires protested loudly as he swung into the drive between a thick grove of bushes.

Something black dashed from behind a clump. The brakes squealed as his foot slammed down, but it was too late. The object careened against the side of the car with a sickening thump.

Kirk was out of the car immediately and looked in horror at the small boy screaming by the side of the drive. He wore a dark jacket and jeans, and for a heart-stopping second, Kirk thought he had hit him. Then he saw that the boy was huddled over a small black dog, and a sigh of relief exploded from him. At least the child hadn't been hit.

He hurried over and squatted down beside him. "Let's see if he's hurt," he urged gently. The tear-stained face looked up at him, and he saw the boy was an Indian.

"Don't touch him!"

The angry order brought Kirk's head snapping up, and he stared over his shoulder. He rose slowly as a woman emerged from the bushes. The slight arch to her nose was nicely balanced by her pronounced cheekbones. A green band circled her forehead, restraining hair as black as sin that hung down her back in a thick braid. Her skin had the smoothness of rich cream, and an eye-catching amount of it was showing. She was dressed in faded cut-off jeans and a green T-shirt. A quick glance showed that her long slim body had all the right curves. But what held Kirk's attention were her eyes. They were the clear intense blue of the New Mexico sky above them—and very, very angry.

She was a glorious Indian goddess, filled with righteous wrath. His stomach muscles tightened in an involuntary reflex. He now knew what it felt like to be poleaxed.

"I'm checking to see how badly the dog's hurt."

She ignored him and dropped on her knees beside the

16

weeping boy as he clutched the dog. "Are you all right, John? Do you hurt anyplace?" she asked anxiously as her hands flew over him, checking for bruises or broken bones. Between sobs, the boy denied being hurt, and she gathered the two in her arms with a sigh of thanksgiving.

"The animal ran from behind the bushes. I didn't have time to stop." It seemed important that she understand that.

The woman's incredible blue eyes blazed at him again. "That was obvious. The way you came tearing in here, it's a miracle you were able to stop at all to see what damage you did."

"I wasn't going that fast."

Her finely arched brows rose higher. "From the screeching your tires made, I'm surprised there's any rubber left on them."

"If there was a decent sign at the entrance, I wouldn't have almost missed the driveway."

"Oh? Now it's the sign's fault. Do you always have excuses for your careless driving?"

Kirk's teeth clenched as he hung on to his temper. She was doing a good job goading him. He was tired and still feeling the shock of the dog thumping against his car. Seeing the huddled boy lying there had cost him a year of his life. "I'm a damn good driver. No one ever complained before."

"Perhaps because they were too terrified to speak."

His breath exploded in exasperation. "Look, I've driven a good thousand miles the past two days and I'm tired. I have no desire to get into a slugging match with you."

The dog, he realized as he looked down, was a puppy. It had recovered from its shock and was licking the tears from the boy's face. Kirk reached for his wallet and pulled out a fifty-dollar bill. "The dog looks okay, but I'd like it to be checked. This should take care of the veterinarian bill."

Her eyes blazed anew. "So now you're trying to salve

17

your conscience with a bribe! You know what you can do with your money!"

His lip curled. "You've got a nasty mouth and mind, lady." He had had enough. She was still holding the boy, soothing him. He thrust the money into the pocket of the boy's jacket. In doing so the back of his hand made contact with the soft swell of her breast, and his fingers rubbed against the warm texture of her arm.

Her lips parted in shock as their eyes met and locked. They stared at each other, unmoving, for a long telling moment.

When the puppy wriggled free and the boy ran happily after it, they were snapped from the spell. Kirk drew in a deep breath. Irrationally irritated, he turned to the Jaguar and found himself cursing under his breath. Without a backward glance, he got in the car and continued down the drive.

The woman wouldn't have affected him like that if he wasn't so tired, he assured himself fiercely. Thinking he'd run over a child hadn't helped his nerves either. He never got involved with married women, and he had no desire to start now. Considering his reaction to that Indian princess, if the good Lord was kind, he'd see to it that she didn't cross his path. Kirk hoped she remained well hidden wherever she worked on the Treemont spread.

He braked in front of the adobe house and willed away the memory of parted soft lips ripe for kissing. The house was built in the style of a Spanish hacienda with a red tile roof and rooms opening onto a large inner court. He remembered with affection the happy times he had spent there. It had always offered a sense of peace and serenity. He could stand a large dose of it at present. He pulled the two suitcases from the trunk of the car and strode to the door festooned with iron grillwork.

Within seconds of using the heavy iron knocker, the door was thrown open. A round-faced Indian woman beamed up at him.

"At last! It's good to see you again, Master Kirk. My, you've turned into a handsome man!"

Kirk dropped the bags and grinned as he swept the woman into his arms. "Maria! The one true love of my life. Tell me that you've missed me."

· The rotund woman giggled as she refastened the knot of hair at the back of her neck loosened by his hug. He guessed the housekeeper was close to seventy, yet her black hair held only a few gray streaks.

"Miss you? Where did you ever get that idea? I can get my work done now that I don't have bruised knees to clean or endless batches of cookies to make. The jar was always mysteriously empty." A mist clouded her dark brown eyes as she examined the tall man before her. "Ah, if your mother could only see the man you have become."

"We'll always miss her," Kirk admitted softly. Then, to avoid the memories crushing down on them, he changed the subject. "I assume Mr. Treemont told you I'd be here for a while. Is he around?"

"He said to give you his apologies. He's involved in one of his golf tournaments and will be here later."

"I guess that means my father is in it also?"

Maria laughed. "What else? Let's hope they're partners. If not, you can be sure there's a battle going on between them to see who wins. Mr. Treemont asked me to tell you that he's giving a small dinner party here tonight and expects you to be there. You know how he loves his parties."

Thinking of his weariness, Kirk grimaced as he picked up the cases. "I remember. Tell me, do I have my old room?"

"Of course. I aired it out myself and made sure it was ready."

Kirk stopped himself from asking if the blue-eyed goddess was from her tribe and was part of the household. He wasn't going to get involved, he reminded himself sternly.

The inner sliding glass doors were open. He left the large foyer where they'd been talking to walk through the

19

central placito on the way to his room. The lush foliage struck him as it always had. The courtyard was an oasis, cool and inviting, a dramatic change from the hot semiarid desert that lay beyond the walls of the house.

Memories had him smiling as he passed the central fountain. Goldfish swam in the basin, identical to the ones that had fascinated him as a child. He could still feel the shock when he'd fallen in once in his need to find out if they were really made of gold.

A wide overhang extended around the four sides of the court, a protection to the rooms overlooking the garden from the burning sun or infrequent rain squalls. He checked the grapes forming on the vines covering the wooden grillwork extending from the overhang. The fruit was partially ripe. They had been his downfall one summer's day when, on a dare, he'd eaten a cluster that wasn't fully ripe. His mouth puckered recalling the tartness and the gagging he'd struggled against showing.

Memories, all long forgotten. He was surprised how they crowded in on him after all these years.

On three sides the house was one story. At the back rose an additional story where the guest rooms were located. Kirk went up the stairs two steps at a time, suddenly eager to see his room. There was a wide window seat that offered an exceptional view of the Sangre de Cristo foothills. As a child, he'd spent hours there, dreaming wonderful, impossible dreams.

The room seemed untouched by time. The walls were the same rough plaster painted white. The drapes and spread on the white painted iron bed were still the green and blue print he remembered. Ever since Charlie Walk-the-Horse had explained what the designs meant on the Navaho rug covering the floor, it had been special.

Good Lord, why all this nostalgia? he wondered as he went to the window. Yes, the view was as he remembered. The red soil was sparsely dotted with silver green bushes. Distance gave the mountains a bluish tint. To the right the two buttes rising starkly from the level ground still looked like forts. Before going to college he had finally fulfilled one of his daydreams and climbed them both.

Hearing joyful yipping, his attention was pulled to the back door where the kitchen garden was planted. A black ball of fur bounced into view. It was the puppy, and Kirk was pleased to see that except for a slight favoring to a front paw, it seemed over its ordeal. The small boy raced after it, shouting happily. Kirk was thankful to see that the tears and the traumatic event were a thing of the past.

Kirk leaned forward, pressing his forehead on the pane of glass. The boy's mother? Was she following to get something from the garden?

A searing oath exploded as he jerked away from the window. He was startled by his eagerness to catch another glimpse of the black-haired woman. She was off limits, he reminded himself grimly, no matter what she did to his libido.

The trouble was, he was exhausted. He'd been tired even before the long, grueling ride. He had had no rest between the last three jobs, and each had been complicated, demanding his total concentration. This vacation was to be his bonus. Instead, here he was, so tired that he'd had no resistance to the overwhelming memories. Weariness had lowered his barriers, which explained his strong reaction to the small boy's mother.

Satisfied with his reasoning, he looked longingly at the bed. A glance at his watch showed he had three hours to take a nap. If he expected to be reasonably coherent at the party that evening, he'd be smart to take advantage of the time.

The cases could be unpacked later, he decided. He stripped quickly, yawned once, and stretched, liking the feel of the cool sheets against his long, hard body. Sleep came immediately.

It was dusk when Kirk woke with a start. The drapes billowed as the refreshingly cool mountain breeze blew in,

21

chilling his flesh. He frowned. The windows had been closed against the heat when he had crawled into bed. A quick check showed that his cases had been unpacked also. He really must have zonked out not to have heard the movements in his room. It was just like Maria, he thought with a smile. He untangled his long limbs from the sheet and rose to take a quick shower and dress for dinner.

Twenty minutes later Kirk adjusted his tie as he made his way across the courtyard to the large living room. It and the dining room were to the left side of the square. The family sleeping quarters were on the opposite side. The kitchen and utility rooms were in the back under the guest rooms, finishing off the square. Bracketing the entrance foyer were a library and a den that had always been Charles's private domain. No one ever entered them without his express permission.

Hearing voices, Kirk paused at the entrance to the living room. He'd always loved it. Although heavy dark beams crossed the ceiling, the room had always seemed airy and welcoming, and the worn but comfortable chairs clustered in small groupings invited tired bodies to relax. He was pleased to see that nothing had been changed since Greta Treemont's death.

A man rose from putting a match to the kindling in the fireplace. Kirk examined his host with affection. Age had whitened his hair and added lines to his face, but he was still a commanding figure.

Charles's face lighted with pleasure when he saw Kirk. "Come in, come in! You're just in time to join us for a drink before everyone descends upon us. God, it's good to see you, lad. What is it, three, four years? Not that your dad doesn't keep me up with what you're doing."

His emotion showed in his firm grasp of Kirk's hand. He clapped him on his back and urged him to the well-stocked bar. "What will it be? If you're man enough, I make a wicked martini."

"I'm willing to take a chance." Kirk grinned. Charles

hadn't changed one iota. A movement in the room caught his attention, and he turned as a woman rose fluidly from a high-backed chair.

Once again Kirk's stomach muscles contracted at the sight of her. Gone were the cut-off jeans, the clinging T-shirt. She was wearing a white Grecian-cut gown that left one arm bare. The fire had caught hold and its flames created glowing highlights on her golden skin. Immediately his fingers tingled with the memory of how soft and silky her skin had felt. The thick braid was coiled in a French knot at the nape of her neck. Was it the weight that tilted her head, or was it breeding? Or was it anger? He met her eyes and grimaced when he realized the blue fire was still blazing. Was she going to turn that unfortunate incident into a vendetta?

More important, who was she?

Charles interrupted his reverie by handing Kirk the drink. "How many years is it since you two last saw each other?" he asked. He was having a difficult time hiding his glee over the reaction between the two. The more sparks, the better, he thought. It was a marked improvement over his daughter's usual serenity. Kirk looked at him blankly, which made him grin inwardly. "Don't you recognize her? This is Charla. Surely, after the way you two used to get into each other's hair, you couldn't have forgotten her!"

"Charla?" Kirk managed, trying to wipe off what he was certain was a silly look of amazement. "This is the brat?"

God, what a thing to say! He watched with a sense of impending disaster as her soft lips parted in a parody of a smile.

"You always *were* fond of that term of endearment, weren't you?"

Kirk managed not to flinch. He raised the glass and took a long sip. This was going to be a long and difficult evening.

CHAPTER TWO

"Kirk Webster?" Charla asked in amazement. She had just finished relating to her father the near catastrophe in the driveway earlier that afternoon, and he'd told her who he imagined the speed demon was.

Charles looked with affection at his daughter. She was a knockout in that dress. If that didn't get things started, he thought, his faith in the younger generation would be destroyed. "Yes. Don't tell me you've forgotten Tyson has a son?"

Her eyes narrowed in instant wariness. "The last time I saw him he was going off to college. When did his hair turn white?" Her lip curled in a faint snarl. "No doubt chasing women got to be too draining."

Her father gave an indulgent shake to his head. "Surely you've outgrown that sniping. For two kids that professed to hate each other, you were inseparable."

"That's because our vacations were long and we had no one else to play with."

He looked at her with gentle reproach in his clear blue eyes. "I thought you loved the place?" He and Tyson had had neighboring ranches, and the kids were always together. But after Sara died, Tyson had sold his ranch and moved to Albuquerque.

"Oh, I did," she admitted hurriedly, seeing his pain. She took a sip from her cocktail and turned the conversation back to the reason for the unexpected guest. "Why is he

24

staying with us? His father lives in Albuquerque and surely would prefer having him stay there."

"It was genes."

Charla looked at him, startled. "What?"

"You wanted to know how Kirk got his white hair. He inherited it from his father. Didn't you know Tyson's hair also changed while he was in college? I believe Kirk's grandfather's did the same thing."

Charles went to the fireplace and extracted a long match from its case. "The guests will be coming soon. I better get this started." The match rasped against the cover and flared to life.

The ignited sulfur emitted a faint acrid odor, making Charla wrinkle her nose. "Why do I have the feeling that you're evading my question? What are you up to, Dad?"

He reached for the poker and made a production of adjusting the logs. Sometimes he wished his daughter wasn't quite so astute. He caught a sound by the door and turned with relief to greet his house guest. Kirk couldn't have timed his entrance more perfectly. "Come in, come in," he called with what he hoped wasn't too obvious eagerness. Lord, he'd grown into a handsome man, Charles thought. What marvelous grandchildren those two would make!

Charla rose slowly from her seat and glared at the intruder with narrowed eyes. Was this another in her father's unceasing efforts to get her married? He was scraping the bottom of the barrel if he thought Kirk would appeal to her!

Charla had been in near panic when she had heard the screech of tires and John's piercing wail. She had raced to the scene, terrified. Her relief had been enormous when she discovered that young John hadn't been hurt. The fluctuation of emotions had left no room to deal with the stranger. Grudgingly, she admitted now to maybe having overreacted when he offered to pay to have the puppy checked, but at the time, it was the best she could do. If she'd known who the arrogant man was, she might have added a few more words.

Examining him now, she realized that she should have recognized his black slashing eyebrows that shadowed those piercing gray eyes. His father had the same features.

Yet time had produced some very basic and telling changes in Kirk. The jeans and golf shirt he'd worn earlier proved that his body was in top condition. But now, seeing him attired in a pale blue jacket and charcoal pants, she had to admit that the picture left from childhood bore little relationship to this vital man.

He'd always been long limbed but solidly built. Lord, she'd butted her head into him enough times to remember that. His chest had broadened, as had his shoulders, and she would bet his stomach was just as hard as it had been.

She used to hate his know-it-all attitude. It manifested itself now in an assurance that he carried with a casualness that had her gritting her teeth. Still, she had to give the devil his due. He'd earned it. From the tales Tyson was happy to divulge, Kirk was extremely successful in a very precarious profession.

His uncalled-for words when realizing who she was had her girding for battle. Brat, indeed! Maria's announcement that the first guests were arriving was the only thing that prevented her from venting her anger. She swept past him with an icy glare and left with her father to welcome the newcomers.

"Stop evading," she hissed behind the smile she kept in place for the guests as they arrived. "Why is he bunking with us?"

Charles's expression was pained. " 'Bunking'? Surely our hospitality hasn't degenerated to *that* level."

"Dad!"

If he didn't know it was physically impossible, he'd have sworn she was breathing fire. He put on his wounded look. "I don't know why you're reacting like this. You know the problem we're having at the plant. In spite of constant inspections, several flawed parts have slipped through. It could ruin the company. Kirk is here to see what's going on. It is, after all, what he specializes in doing. Naturally, I invited him to stay with us. His father's place would add unnecessary commuting miles. I never imagined you'd find cause to take issue with it."

Charla readjusted her smile to greet the new arrivals. When they were aimed to the bar, she returned to the argument. "He'd be closer to the plant if he stayed in town."

"Charla!" Shock underlined the exclamation. "How could you even think that? Surely those childhood arguments you two specialized in have been long buried." He exhaled an exasperated sigh. "I told him he was crazy when he suggested staying in town. I pointed out that this was the week of the big powwow. He'd be lucky to find a broom closet to rent. What's the matter with you two? Don't ties of old friends and common hospitality mean anything to your generation?"

He looked bewildered and hurt and Charla felt foolish. He was right. Why was she making such an issue over Kirk's staying with them? Her suspicion that the two parents were plotting something more outrageous than usual evidently had no basis in fact. Her father seldom brought business problems home, but she was well aware of his concern about that government contract. It would have been odd, indeed, if Kirk had stayed anyplace but with them. During childhood this had been his second home.

"Isn't Tyson coming?" she asked in surprise as they went to mingle with the guests.

"He said he'd be a little late but would get here before we sat down to eat. He's bringing Sandy Marlowe. Her children were with her for the day. They're late going home, so she asked for extra time to get ready. Between you and me, he needs that time to get over the trouncing I gave him," he added with relish.

27

Seeing his smirk, Charla laughed. "You two! Don't you ever get tired of showing each other up?"

Charles grinned sheepishly. "He won the first two rounds. I intend to enjoy today's victory."

She shook her head with affection and went to check with Maria to make sure that everything was well in the kitchen. Her gaze went over the guests. She knew them all and saw that they were already enjoying themselves. It was going to be a good party.

Her perusal stopped when she saw Kirk. Now that her anger had faded she could appreciate the man he'd become. Without doing anything to draw attention, he still stood out in the crowd. A small frown furrowed her brow. Three wives who had reputations for prowling evidently thought so, too. They were clustered around him, and from their laughter, they were finding conversation with him highly entertaining.

He glanced up as if he were aware of her examination. Pewter eyes locked with blue for what could have been no more than a second before one of the women drew his attention back to her.

Charla drew in a slow careful breath to ease the sudden tightness in her chest. It had been a neutral look. There had been no heat of anger, no cold accusation, so why the reaction? There'd been nothing more than a promise.

Promise? She laughed uncomfortably while continuing to the kitchen. Where did that crazy idea come from? Her conscience must be on a guilt trip over the tart rejoiners she'd thrown at him to dredge up something like that!

Joe Letterman was waiting for her with two cocktails when she emerged from the kitchen. "Can't have our charming hostess without a drink." He smiled with appreciation as his gaze slid over her dress. "I take those words back. 'Charming' is too insipid. 'Sexy,' 'breathtaking,' 'gorgeous,' states it better."

Charla smiled and tasted the drink before answering. "You do know how to make a woman feel special." Joe

28

had been promoted to supervisor at the plant when her father had been made chairman of the board. She liked him for the deference he showed her father. They had a nice easy relationship, dating occasionally, mainly when needing a partner for various social functions.

"Haven't you heard?" he replied lightly. "You are a very special lady." A maid stopped with a tray of hors d'oeuvres. He took a cracker topped with cream cheese and caviar and popped it into her mouth. "Do I get points for remembering how you like the stuff?"

With his hand curled around her elbow, he urged her toward two men in a heated discussion. "That looks like it needs to be defused. I was behind them when they arrived. It was obvious they already had several drinks in them. Maybe we better see about separating them."

Charla liked his concern and her gaze was warm. "Thanks, Joe. They're great fun except when they forget to count how many drinks they've had."

He returned her smile. His hand was draped casually at her waist while they talked to the angry men.

"That's Joe Letterman."

Kirk raised a brow at Charles's observation. He'd managed to elude the women and return to his host.

"The man with Charla," Charles beamed. He'd spotted Kirk eyeing the two and decided to grab the opportunity to stir things a little. Tyson had better hurry if he wanted to be in on all the fun, he thought. "He's in charge of the plant, now that I've been pushed up on the board. He's a good fellow. I wouldn't be surprised if there might be wedding bells in the near future. Come along so I can introduce you. You'll be working together on this thing."

"I assume he knows that you've called me in?" The man's hand looked possessive the way it rested on the curve of Charla's slim waist. Charles could be right. The smiles they'd exchanged had been warm enough.

"Of course. He's just as anxious to get to the bottom of

the problem as the board. He's no fool. If the plant folds, he's out of a job."

And loses the daughter? Kirk frowned at the uncharitable thought. "Does he have any idea how it's being done?"

"Not as of the last time we talked."

"Maybe we three should get together later and discuss what's going on."

Charles looked at him with horror. "This is a party, a time to relax. He suggested the two of you have lunch tomorrow."

Kirk's look was scathing. "Lunch? You mean I gave up my vacation to come here, and he's obliging me by finding time to discuss this over lunch? From the way Tyson acted, this was a situation that needed to be resolved immediately. What's going on here?"

Kirk's barely contained anger had Charles shifting uneasily. "Take it easy, son. We had no idea when you'd get here. I'm sure Joe will see you first thing in the morning if that's what you want."

"That's what I want," he replied firmly. Letterman's hand, he saw in irritation, was now resting on the nape of her neck as they made their way to another group of guests. "I have hopes of getting this solved quickly so I can still get in some of my vacation."

"Of course, of course," Charles soothed him. "Come, we'll tell Joe about the change."

Kirk found he didn't particularly want to meet Letterman just then. The man might find his hand crushed when it was offered. He found himself draining his drink and handing the glass to a passing waiter for a refill. He followed Charles reluctantly to where Charla and her companion were standing talking to another guest. He was not happy with what was going on inside him. In fact, he had a surprising desire to get in his Jaguar and race back to New Orleans to the lovely and safe Creole lady.

From his dark hair and eyes and swarthy complexion, Kirk guessed the man had Indian blood in him. As did

Charla. Was that a factor in their attraction? Greta had been one quarter Navaho. It was from her that Charla had inherited the black hair, honey skin, and striking bone structure. Her eyes, though, were the intense blue of her father's. The combination in their daughter was enough to make any man catch his breath.

Charla watched the two men walk toward them. She still had difficulty accepting this new Kirk. He came with a slow loping gait that reminded her of an outdoorsman. A memory, long forgotten, flashed in her mind.

The cowboys on the ranch had rounded up several wild horses, and Kirk and Charla had been taken by a young filly. Somewhere they'd come up with the idea that if they broke her, their parents would let them keep her. With carrots and sugar stolen from the kitchen plus infinite patience, they'd gained a grudging acceptance by the animal. Their excitement could hardly be contained when she didn't fight the bridle, and then the day finally came when Kirk decided to ride her. The cowhands were off doing their chores, and their parents were safely in the house. He slid on the filly's back and nervously tightened his hand on the rope. The animal astonished them by not moving, and Kirk had flashed her a smile of triumph. Then all hell broke loose. The horse leapt straight into the air and twisted violently before coming down on its feet. Charla remembered her awe when she saw Kirk sail off into space as if possessing wings. He had landed with a bone-crushing jolt and lain unmoving in the dust.

Completely horrified, Charla had squeezed through the fence and flown to his side. Weeping helplessly, she'd pulled his head against her childish breast. She had rained kisses on his face, begging him not to die. He finally opened his eyes and looked at her. No words were spoken as he raised a dusty hand and brushed at the tears with a strange gentleness. Then white-faced parents raced to the corral, and the small sweet moment of communication was over.

31

Strange how she'd forgotten the event until now. Kirk stopped before her and watched her with a strange look. She realized she'd been staring at him. "I was remembering something." The memory was still strong and she wondered if he ever thought of it. "Remember when you tried to ride that wild horse and nearly got killed?"

His eyes darkened and she wondered if he were recalling the tender moment they had shared. It was more likely that the aching muscles took precedence—and the scoldings that they had managed to survive.

"What brought that up?" Charles groaned. "When we heard those screams coming from the corral, we were certain one of you had been killed by a horse. Sometimes we wondered how you two survived the crazy things you dreamed up.

"You'll have to ask Charla to give you the full story one day, and you'll see what I mean," Charles informed Joe, seeing his confusion. "Meanwhile, I want you to meet Kirk Webster. He's the man I was telling you about. He wants to meet with you first thing in the morning so he can get started. He's giving up vacation time and would like to get this solved so he can still get in some R and R."

"No problem. Will nine do? That will give me time to clear the worst of the problems that always seem to be waiting each morning."

Kirk did not crush Joe's offered hand. In fact, he decided he could even like the man. "Nine will be fine. I'll want a tour of the plant also."

"That's easily arranged. I'll have a badge made for you so you have the freedom of the place. I'm with you—the quicker this is solved, the happier I'll be. After all the time I've put in trying to figure out where we slipped up, I might even claim some R and R for myself."

His smile included Charla, a fact that Kirk did not miss.

Maria announced that dinner was ready, and the twelve people went into the dining room.

Kirk had always liked the room. The long Spanish mis-

32

sion oak table gleamed from faithful waxing, and excellent paintings by local artists gave color to the whitewashed adobe. He even recognized the linen place mats as ones his parents had given Charles and Greta one long-ago Christmas.

Memories. The place was flooded with them. Even Charla had been caught up with them. Imagine her remembering that accident. He couldn't recall the last time that he had. For a fleeting second, he again saw her tear-stained face. In spite of the pain that was breaking through the shock, an unexpected moment of tenderness, a need to reassure her, had overtaken him. He'd been overwhelmed by the realization that in spite of their constant bickering, she really liked him and was frightened that he might die.

As hostess, Charla sat at the foot of the table. He and Letterman were seated on either side of her. Kirk ate hungrily. In a desire to put the miles behind him, he'd stopped for unsatisfying meals at fast food places. Around him the other men were involved in rehashing the golf tournament that was still going on. The conversation centered on the various plays, and since the women were golfers also, he soon gave up any pretense of following it.

"You don't play?" Charla asked sympathetically when she saw his withdrawal.

"Occasionally, but not with this dedication. Do you?"

"Occasionally. When I have some time."

He tasted the wine and smiled over the rim of the glass. "Do you ever have the feeling our fathers think we're barbarians because of our lack of interest?"

"Frequently." She smiled indulgently to where her father was in heated debate with Tyson. He'd arrived as promised shortly before Maria's announcement. He had just had time to greet his son and introduce the vivacious woman with him.

"And with what do you occupy your time?"

"She works helping my people," Joe inserted. "Which reminds me, Charla, Mary White Feather doesn't know if

33

she can finish any more paintings right now. I told her you'd get in touch with her."

Kirk felt annoyed at the adroit way he'd been nudged out as they discussed the problem of Mary White Feather. He turned to the woman sitting at his other side who had been hinting for his attention. She was into horses, and he dredged up an interest in the subject for the rest of the meal.

He and Charla didn't speak again until the dinner was over and the guests drifted back to the living room where after-dinner liqueurs were served. Charla managed to slip away from the unusual way Joe was monopolizing her time with the excuse that she had to see to the other guests. If he wasn't such a good friend, she would have been annoyed by his sudden possessiveness.

Kirk watched her move gracefully from one group to the other, checking that the drinks were right or subtly shifting an ashtray closer to a careless hand. Gone was the long-legged tagalong brat that had been the bane of his existence growing up. Surely he wouldn't have gotten into so many scrapes if she hadn't been there goading him on.

His nap had taken the edge off his tiredness, but now, sated with a full stomach, it returned. Admittedly, the amount of wine he'd imbibed wasn't helping, but Charles had always had a superlative wine cellar. Kirk sauntered out to the placito, leaving the talk and tobacco smoke behind, and took a deep breath of fresh air. He'd give it another half hour and then make his excuses, he decided. The bed was definitely beckoning.

The subdued lighting among the shrubs cast interesting shadows in the courtyard. He walked the flagstone paths, his mind pleasantly blank. He inhaled the faint pungent aroma of the petunias planted around the fountain. Seeing an iron bench on the far side, he went to sit down on it. He reached absently for a cigarette and recalled that he hadn't replenished his supply. Perhaps this was as good a time as any to try and quit. Again.

A movement by the door caught his attention, and he looked up to see Charla approach through the diamond-dusted spray from the fountain. Backlighted by the glow from the room, he was caught by the gently rounded curves of her silhouette. Yes, the brat was no more. This was a woman who could cause a man to dream.

He walked slowly around the fountain to her. In unguarded repose, he could see that she, too, was tired. She stood with eyes closed and didn't see him when he stopped a few feet from her.

"It appears that hostessing isn't the easy job you make it seem."

Her eyes flew open in surprise. "It's been a long day."

"For me, too. Fortunately, I can beg off and make it to bed in a few minutes, but I guess you're committed to stay until the last person leaves."

Her smile was wry. "All too true. But I assume that they'll be leaving shortly. Tomorrow is the final round in the tournament, and they'll want to be alert to give it their best."

A cloud moved on, unveiling the half-moon. She was silver and dark shadows. His hand moved without conscious thought. His fingers did what they'd wanted to do ever since seeing her near the driveway. The soft caress started at her shoulder and slid slowly down to her elbow and back again.

"Your skin feels just like I thought it would. Smooth satin." His voice deepened as his eyes anchored her, denying her movement.

"That's a creditable endorsement for the body lotion I use. Do you mind if I send that statement to the manufacturer?"

His hand paused for a moment in its glide over her shoulder. Body? For a disturbing instant, he imagined her silken softness pressed against him completely. "My dear Charla, I'm willing to give them all the endorsement they wish."

"No!" They both knew her breathless denial was already too late. This was the only culmination possible to what had started when they'd met that afternoon. His other hand raised to cup her face as the distance between them disappeared. She grabbed his wrists with the full intention of pushing him away, but she was curiously drained of the energy to do so.

Her lips were still parted in protest when his took them for his own. They had a rich lushness and tasted faintly of wine. Some part of him protested, told him not to be foolish, but he was already drunk with the taste. Her perfume, smelling faintly of violets, became his with each breath. But beneath it was the essence of her, the feminine musk that he knew at some subliminal level he'd never forget.

Neither could speak when at last he raised his head. They stared at each other with guarded eyes until her gaze drifted over his shoulder as if no longer able to meet the flame in his.

She stiffened and pulled away from him. "You—you unspeakable beast!" she hissed. Anger wiped away the passion, and he stared in amazement at the fury in her eyes.

"What are you talking about?"

"Don't deny it! You set this up with our parents. Did you think all you had to do was appear with your broad shoulders and handsome good looks and I'd fall for you? How low can you all get!"

His hands went to her shoulders as she started to turn away. "Are we talking the same language?" he asked in confusion.

"Your innocent act doesn't hold water. Just look at our gloating parents. My father has put me through some pretty horrid farces trying to get me married, but this is the lowest one yet."

Kirk looked over his shoulder into the living room. She was right. The two men were standing by the fireplace, their attention focused on their children. And, yes, their expressions were disgustingly gloating. While the lighting was dim in the court, he and Charla weren't exactly hidden.

He swore and his anger matched hers. "If you think that kiss was on command from those old coots, you need your head examined. As for marriage," he raged, "you have my full assurance that marrying you is the last thing on my mind! I'm going to pretend I never met you. And you better believe that tomorrow I'll be out of this crazy house!"

He stormed across the courtyard and took the stairs to his room two at a time.

CHAPTER THREE

Charla stared at Kirk's retreating back as he disappeared up the stairs. Kirk's anger left her feeling scorched and uncomfortably off balance. Had the constant running battle with her father over getting married made her jump to wrong conclusions?

She looked at the two men toasting each other by the fireplace. No, their satisfaction was obvious. And premature. But Kirk's explosion reassured her. As children, they had constantly been on opposite sides of an issue. But in this, thank heavens, it appeared that they were together. Her breath released in exasperation. She loved the "old coots," as Kirk had called them, but she admitted to doing her own gloating over the downfall of their plotting. Perhaps this time it would teach them a lesson not to interfere with something that was her decision alone.

She returned to her hostess duties, wishing guiltily that the guests would make signs of leaving. She'd had a full day and thought longingly of her bed.

"Where's Kirk? Tyson hasn't had a chance to say more than hello to his son."

Her father's look was innocent, but she'd been the recipient of it too often to be fooled. "Kirk? I don't know . . . Is he missing? Oh, I guess he went to his room. I ran into him in the placito. Something was in his eye. I tried to get it out, but the light was too poor to see."

That should provide them with a reason for seeing them

standing so closely together and give them cause to doubt what they'd seen in the shadowy courtyard. She managed to hide her satisfaction at the two men's crestfallen expressions. They retreated in confusion, leaving Charla smiling grimly. Chalk up one for her side.

Charla breathed an unconscious sigh of relief when she entered the dining room early the next morning where her father was hurrying through breakfast. There was no sign of their house guest. Maybe she was lucky, and he was already gone as he had threatened. Then she was disgusted over her wariness. This was her home, for heaven's sake! *He* was intruding on *her* territory.

"Early teeing off time?" she asked while pouring coffee into a cup.

"Yes, eight thirty. You just missed Kirk. He wanted a quick look over the plant before his meeting with Joe, so I called the watchman to let him in."

She waited with cup poised for the next explosion and looked at her father in surprise when he returned to the newspaper propped by his plate. Surely Kirk's moving out would cause more of a reaction. Her eyes narrowed in speculation. Could it be that the rat had changed his mind? Damn, just when she thought she was home free with him gone. What did she have to do to get him to leave?

She was suddenly aware of the heated cup resting on her lip, and it was lowered quickly to the saucer. The warmth triggered the memory of another heat when his mouth had taken possession of hers.

"Do you think he has the knowledge to help unravel what's going on at the plant?" she asked to eradicate the sensation.

Charles scraped remnants of butter from his plate and smoothed it over the last of his English muffin. "The board is behind him one hundred percent."

That didn't impress her. They were all yes-men as far as she could tell and would never vote down anything

Charles Treemont decided was best. "I know in your eyes that as Tyson's son, Kirk can do no wrong. But I've always been suspicious about his sudden departure from the FBI. All I heard for years was how he loved his work and his rapid promotions. Then overnight he quit, according to him, to start his own business."

Charles's blue eyes held anger as he stared at her in disbelief. "I won't waste a comment on what you're inferring. However, I will remind you that his company has an excellent track record or it never would have been considered, friend or not. The future of the plant is too important to me to risk playing games. Don't forget that I know every person who works there. Some whole families are in our employ. Do you think I'd put their jobs, their livelihood, on the line for a whim?"

She squirmed inwardly. The chastisement was deserved. "I'm sorry. I guess I'm still tired and not thinking clearly."

He gazed astutely at her bowed head. "Are you sure that's the reason? Or are you stuck with reacting as you did as a child? I've always been proud of your intelligence. Use it now. Kirk is no longer the boy you used to love to tease. Don't you think it's time to bury whatever hatchet you're still clinging to and treat him like the responsible man he's proved himself to be?"

Charla cleared her dry throat. "You're right, Dad. I'll make the effort."

"Good." He drained his cup and rose to place a kiss on the top of her head. "Try it. You might find you like it."

He left the room, and Charla sagged in the chair. She gazed at the stack of buckwheat pancakes Maria put before her with a decided lack of appetite. They were her favorite, and the housekeeper periodically pampered her by making them. Any attempt to refuse them would raise awkward questions. She reached resignedly for the maple syrup.

She turned her thoughts firmly to Mary White Feather, an unschooled but gifted artist. Her paintings were sold through The Trading Post, the consignment store Charla

40

had started for the Indians. She and Mary were the same age and had become good friends. The problem was that Mary's husband, usually a wonderful, caring man, periodically indulged in alcohol. When that occurred, the children were sent to relatives and Mary remained to take care of him while stoically fending off his abuse. Charla knew from past experiences that no painting would be done while he was on one of his bouts.

Since the start of the week-long powwow, the shelves of The Trading Post had needed constant replenishing. Satisfied customers from years past had returned to make additional purchases, as had tourists who learned by word of mouth of the store's reputation for top-quality Indian products. The Trading Post had built a steady and faithful following. Mary White Feather's paintings always sold well. Maybe she'd better go to the reservation and see if there were any that were close to being ready for sale, Charla told herself.

She pushed from the table, only then realizing that the pancakes were eaten. She frowned. It appeared that as long as she kept Kirk out of her mind, she was fine. It was with commendable restraint that she refrained from questioning Maria if Kirk had asked her to pack his belongings. Maybe he planned to leave after his meeting with Joe. She should be so lucky!

After a quick stop at The Trading Post to check if Rosemary Downs, her assistant, had enough help, Charla continued on to the Santa Clara Pueblo where Mary lived. Her van acquired another coating of dust as she threaded the rutted dirt road to the small nondescript house. It had no redeeming features, but she noticed that both it and the sweat lodge a short distance from it were in good repair. When not under the influence of alcohol, Mary's husband was a caring man. It made it more understandable why Mary tolerated his irrational behavior.

Mary met her at the door. She wore the colorful long-sleeved dress the women preferred when on their own

41

land. There was a sullen look of defiance on her face. Charla respected her pride and tried not to wince when she noticed the bruise discoloring one eye.

"Hello, Mary. I have good news for you. Your last two paintings have been sold. I'm here on the off chance that you might have some others ready."

They'd gone through this small face-saving exchange before. It was to alert Mary that there was money for her to pick up if she needed it. If not, they banked it for her until her husband was over his seasonal problem. Otherwise, he'd demand it from her and continue drinking his way into oblivion.

Mary's expression relaxed. "I do have three paintings ready for framing. I just haven't had the time to get to do it."

"Johnny would be happy to do that for you. He knows how you like them done." Johnny was the handyman at the post. He was a jewel, capable and willing to do the myriad of odd jobs that running a place like The Trading Post entailed.

The woman hesitated a moment, calculating if she wanted to pay for the work. But she knew from experience that sales were made when the town was flush with tourists.

"All right. Come, I'll show you."

Her husband had built her a small studio behind the house. She unlocked the door, and Charla was struck once again over the trouble he'd gone to to put in the bank of windows on the north side so she'd have the necessary light.

A partially finished painting sat on the easel, but Charla's attention went to the three lining the wall. Strong. Powerful. Those were the words that always came to her mind when encountering one of Mary's paintings. While the colors were subtle, they held a vibrancy that caught and held the eye. Mary's favorite subjects were the land she loved and knew so well and the people around her.

Two were of children caught in thoughtful repose. Charla knew immediately that there would be no trouble selling them.

The third was of her husband. Mary painted as she saw things. There was no softening of the worry lining his face or the signs of dissipation. But his eyes held a love, a commitment, that made Charla catch her breath. Was that what Mary saw in him, what kept her by his side, taking his abuse when nursing him through his relapses?

Charla knew that she had to own it. If she ever found a man who looked at her that way, she'd hold on and cherish him and never let him go. There would be no need for her father to parade any more men for her inspection.

"These are *marvelous,* Mary! I keep thinking you've reached your pinnacle, but each time you stretch further."

A quiet pleasure glowed in the woman's dark eyes. "I felt good while painting them."

"It shows. I'll take them now. There are some blankets in the van to wrap around them so they won't get damaged. Do you know if Tallfellow has any pottery ready? I could take it now and save him a trip into town."

"I heard he fired the kiln the other day. They should be finished by now."

"Good. I'll stop by and check."

They took the paintings outside and wrapped them carefully. Before driving away, Charla saw Mary's husband weaving uncertainly as he came to the doorway. His hair was matted and his clothes rumpled. It was difficult to equate him with the man in the painting.

She felt a deep sadness. Her mother had been one quarter Navaho, and Charla shared a heritage with these Indians. She knew all too well the frustration, the depression, that drove the Indians to find escape in drink. In her small way, she was doing what she could for them by giving them a place through which they could sell their art and thereby regain some of their battered pride.

Upon returning from college, Charla had been certain

43

her training as a social worker would help make a difference. She soon found she was stifled working through the limiting structure of the Indian welfare system. When her father suggested a store where the Indians could bring their work on consignment, she had jumped on the idea. It had proved successful, and she got pieces from some of the best artists in the area. When larger and more prestigious galleries offered to give any of them a showing, she was the first to cheer these local artists on to bigger and better exposure.

Her lips pursed as she drove on. When working for the FBI had Kirk also chafed under the suffocating weight of paperwork, the unbending rules that came down from bosses long out of the field? She'd soon grown to hate the frustration from edicts that had only succeeded in making a difficult situation harder to deal with. The thought made her squirm when recalling her not-so-subtle accusation at breakfast. Her father had jumped on her with good cause.

And what was Kirk doing center front in her mind again? He'd been successfully banished while she was concentrating on The Trading Post. It was time to switch back to it again.

Would he have taken his luggage and left by the time she returned home? The golf tournament would be over and the awards dinner would be held that evening. Joe had asked her to attend with him, but she'd begged off, knowing she'd be tired from working at The Trading Post. Perhaps she should have accepted. That way she'd avoid contact with her old nemesis.

And, dammit, what was he doing back in her thoughts again?

"Are you sure you don't want to come?" Charles asked her as they met in the living room later that evening. "With the amount of food I saw being delivered to the club, one more won't make any difference."

Charla shook her head. "Frankly, I'm bushed. I went to

Santa Clara and brought back a batch of pottery. We barely had time to get it unpacked. Most was sold before it got on the shelves."

The lines between his eyes deepened. "Sounds like you've got a good thing going there. But do you need to work so hard? That's not why I cheered you on about starting the store."

"It's just this week. You know the influx of tourists that we get with one of these powwows." She smiled with affection as her father brought her a drink. He was still strikingly handsome, especially in the semiformal navy jacket and cream-colored slacks.

"How did it go today? Any spectacular shots?"

Charles expelled a long sigh. "They were spectacular enough. Two in sand traps and three in the rough. But I got them back on the green without any trouble."

Did she dare ask how Tyson had fared? They'd been partners in the tournament, so the combined score was what counted. "Are you up for a prize this time?"

"Maybe. But I doubt any of the top ones."

"That will please Maria," she smiled goadingly. "She won't have to search for a place to put another huge trophy." The top shelf in his den was crowded with evidence of his prowess on the greens.

He grinned back at her. "Well, if I can't get you to change your mind, I better get going. At least Kirk won't be alone. He begged off coming, and I felt guilty about leaving him behind, although he said he was tired and planned to go to bed early. I needn't tell you to extend the usual Treemont hospitality."

Her heart did an unusual flip. "There goes my plan to have a tray in front of the fireplace and go to bed early."

He took a healthy swallow of his drink to hide his pleasure. "You can still do that. Two trays in front of the fire, I mean. Kirk looks like he could use some relaxing. Maria wouldn't object."

Charla could think of a long list of objections.

Her glance went to the second floor as she crossed the courtyard to her room. The drapes were drawn, but light glowed through the fabric. So the mighty Kirk was back. Maybe she could talk Maria into fixing trays for both of them so they could eat in their own rooms.

The idea had favor until she realized that he'd no doubt look at it as if she were hiding. It didn't please her to know that he could be right. Pride made her throw away the idea. Surely she could survive one meal alone with him, for heaven's sake!

Her thoughts were black as she stepped into the shower. Why was she making such a big deal of sharing a meal? He wasn't about to bite her! She rubbed her arm unconsciously and looked down, startled. There had been bruises there at one time, double arcs made by teeth.

She grimaced, remembering how she had howled. It had been as much from pain as the surprise that he'd retaliated in kind. She had been barely five and could recall the frustration but not the reason. Kirk had been ignoring her, as usual, and she'd bitten his hand. His eyes had blazed with anger, causing her to quake even as she glared at him in defiance. The next thing she knew he'd sunk his white teeth into her arm. She'd never again used that means of getting his attention.

Kirk was at the liquor cabinet mixing a drink when she entered the living room. She'd put on well-washed jeans and a casual shirt in a defiance she refused to acknowledge. It annoyed her to see his dress was similar.

He was in partial profile and hadn't heard her. It gave Charla time to examine him in repose. Tired lines carved his face, augmenting the excuse he'd given her father. Too much burning the candle at both ends, she decided in derision, ignoring the memory of Tyson's comments about the tough cases he'd been involved in.

"I'll have the same if that's vodka you're using."

He glanced over his shoulder and gave her a slight nod.

So it was going to be that way, was it? She didn't feel like talking either.

He handed her the martini silently and selected a chair opposite her to sink into. He sighed after taking a sip and leaned his head back on the cushion. His eyes closed, and she stared at him in irritation before giving a dismissing shrug. Maria would announce dinner in half an hour. It had been a crowded day, and she, too, could benefit from some quiet relaxation. His day had no doubt been just as busy. One didn't just walk into a problem and expect to solve it without a lot of heavy digging.

"Do you have any clue about how the rejected pieces got shipped out?" She'd been determined not to start the conversation and frowned in disgust at the question.

"The how is easy. They were packed and sent parcel post in the usual way. It's the why and who that will take time."

His eyes remained closed, and she watched as he reached for his drink on the table and took a sip without spilling a drop. Fascinated, she closed her eyes to see if her coordination was as well honed. Her hand searched slowly for the glass. A soft "Damn!" escaped as her fingers dipped into the chilled liquid. She reached in annoyance for a napkin. It was fortunate that she didn't see the amusement glinting in his eyes.

Kirk had used his long lashes to advantage before. They were effective shields when he slitted his eyes. He hadn't meant to sit across from her. She'd flitted all too often through his mind that day, interfering with his concentration. He'd just as soon not have her in such clear view.

He had watched her reach for the glass with her eyes closed, wondering what she was doing. Then memory opened. How many times had that monkey imitated what he was doing? Her aping had usually fed his ego, although there had been times he'd been irritated. Could it be that she hadn't outgrown that habit? Something warm flowed through him, and it had nothing to do with the drink he was tasting.

The door chimes rang, and Charla looked up in surprise. "I better answer that. Maria will be busy. Expecting anyone?" she asked. When he shook his head she left the room.

She chose the covered walk skirting the patio to get to the entrance foyer. She used the peephole and pulled the door open with an exclamation.

"Why, hello, Joe. Dad has already left. Were you supposed to go to the club together?" She stepped back so he could come in and had to admire how the cream-colored jacket and pale blue slacks complemented his dark complexion.

"No. I met him there. When he said you weren't coming, I decided to see if I could persuade you to change your mind." He didn't add that the knowledge that Kirk was remaining behind also had prodded him into action.

Charla looked at him in surprise. Their dates had been casual at best. Why this sudden interest? "You should have called and saved yourself the trip. I told Dad I planned an early night. I've had a long and tiring day at The Trading Post."

His gaze went from her to the courtyard beyond and back again. "Are you certain I can't make you change your mind?"

She looked at him, disconcerted by his suddenly harsh expression. He was unexpectedly close, and when his hands gripped her shoulders she frowned in annoyance. "Joe? What—"

"Maybe this will do the trick." Then his mouth was on hers.

Surprise immobilized her, giving him time to pull her close. What had gotten into him? They'd exchanged an occasional kiss after a pleasant evening together, but there had never been this show of passion.

She managed to arch her back and turn her face away

48

from his. "What in the world has gotten into you? Let me go, Joe!" She did not struggle, but her blazing eyes revealed her anger unmistakably.

His cheeks were ruddy under his dark skin, his eyes sullen as he slowly released her. Charla's first reaction was regret. She had enjoyed their dates because they'd been free of this display. There would be no more of them, however.

"It's time you became aware of what you do to me," he muttered thickly. "I tried playing the game your way, but a man can take just so much without exploding."

She blinked. Game? What game? "From your actions, I assume you've had more than one drink, but I think it's best if you leave without saying another word."

He stared belligerently over her shoulder but left without another word. Only after the door was locked behind him did she turn and see what Joe had glared at. Kirk stood at the door to the foyer, sipping his cocktail.

She seethed at his amused look. This she didn't need on top of the fiasco she had just suffered through. "I suppose it was too much for you to respect my privacy?"

"No more than you once did with mine."

Her eyes widened, and he knew she was remembering. He had been all of twelve and he'd cornered the gardener's daughter behind the barn. He'd been fantasizing for a week what it would be like to kiss her. He had been surprised by her willingness and, he admitted later, her expertise that far outstripped his. When he'd come up for air, his emotions in a painful turmoil, two large blue eyes had been staring at him with blatant curiosity. His embarrassment was acute, and he found relief in a searing fury. Charla! He had thought the brat safely in the kitchen helping Maria bake cookies. "You were the worst Peeping Tom." Her grin reminded him of her father's when plotting some new mischief.

Charla recalled how he'd chased her, but she was certain he'd never tried cornering that flirt again.

"It was my first realization that kissing could be more than a peck on the cheek or forehead." Her grin widened impudently. "Or the important part hands could play. Do you know I wondered for at least a week if that was why her, er, development was so advanced."

"God, you were a brat!" Had she really observed that first awkward groping?

"And just think, you were my role model. I figured anything you could do, I could do also."

His black brows lowered in a frown. She'd only been eight. Who the hell had she been experimenting with and kissing at that tender age?

Maria came to tell them dinner was ready, and Charla swept by him to the dining room, a suspicious smile on her face. His frown deepened until he remembered there hadn't been any other children at the ranch. The brat was handing him one—as usual.

When the bell had rung, he'd been concerned about who the evidently unexpected visitor was and had followed her, just in case. He stared at the fragile glass in his hand. Recalling his reaction when seeing the clinch in the foyer, it was surprising the glass hadn't snapped in two. It was a good thing her arms hadn't gone around Letterman. Considering the emotions exploding in him, Letterman would have been lucky to escape with nothing more than a broken jaw.

He flexed his body, easing tense muscles banding his shoulders. Charla walked across the placito, and he watched the sway of her slim hips in the snug jeans, the sweet curve to her rounded bottom. What in the world was he getting into? A smart man knew when to pack and run.

Instead he drained the glass and followed her. He had to admit she'd put a lot of spark into his childhood memories. He'd been there less than two days, and those sparks were again in evidence. Maybe it was destined that they have a second round.

CHAPTER FOUR

Tyson grinned at Charles as they went to the head table and accepted identical trophies and split the prize money. "I'm considering adding a room on the house so I can properly display all these god-awful things," he said wryly.

As they returned to their table, Charles waved the trophy to several well-wishing friends. "Don't let it go to your head. We won only third place."

"Sad but true. There's an awful lot of young bucks whose main ambition seems to give us a hard time." They'd been an unbeatable team for years.

They sat down to the cheers from the guests at their table. Tom Baswell had ordered champagne for a toast. They joined the laughter over his risqué innuendos about their prowess on and off the greens.

"At least he hasn't taken out the latest pictures of his grandson," Tyson commented sotto voce when attention returned to the rest of the awards.

"The evening isn't over yet," Charles reminded him gloomily.

"Talking about grandchildren, how goes it with our own offspring?"

Charles beamed. "Perfect. Couldn't be better."

His friend leaned forward eagerly. "What's happened? Did they go out to dinner together?"

"Better. They're home alone having dinner by the fireplace."

51

"Ah, excellent! If Kirk is anything like his dad, he won't let such a golden opportunity go to waste."

"This is only the opening phase," Charles warned. "I was surprised to discover that there's still some antagonism between them. I had no idea how much they scored off each other when they were children—and how much of it is left to color their thinking."

It was Tyson's turn to beam. "Better still. Kirk thrives on challenges."

They joined the applause for their lucky friend who had won a silver bowl for a hole in one. "Do you buy Charla's explanation of what we saw last night?" Charles asked.

Tyson's shoulders rose in a slight shrug. "Your daughter certainly inherited your ability to tell a story with a straight face. The light in the placito was pretty dim, but it looked authentic to me. As far as I'm concerned, they were kissing. When do you think we can start planning the wedding?"

"I was thinking this fall. The weather will be more agreeable, and most of our friends will be back from their summer vacations."

Tyson nodded in agreement. "Sounds reasonable. I always liked outdoor weddings. I wonder who we should contact about a tent? I have to remember to tell my gardener to work on the lawn so it will be in top condition."

Charles stiffened as if stung. "As father of the bride, I have the final decision over where it will be held."

"I know that, but any fool can see that the space behind my house is perfect for the tents. You've left your land in a natural state. I can't see the guests appreciating the dust they're bound to kick up while stumbling around the sagebrush. Besides, what could be more perfect than their vows being said in that little gazebo of mine? Can't you see it banked with flowers?"

Charles could, but it wasn't in his nature to give in without a fight. Craftily, he could see down the line that acquiescence on this point would be a powerful trump card in his hand for something he wanted.

"Charla might insist that the marriage be held in church," he grumbled slyly.

A slightly gnarled hand waved dismissingly. "She'll probably be concentrating on her trousseau."

Charles pursed his lips in doubt. He was proud of his daughter's appearance, but he couldn't recall her ever enthusing about shopping. But Tyson could be right. A trousseau was different. Meanwhile, they could relieve her of the tedious details of planning the wedding.

"We almost had a complication."

Tyson looked at him with concern. "What do you mean?"

"Something had me call the plant. You know how Della is always on top of everything. I thought I'd check in on how the meeting went between Kirk and Joe."

He had hired Della Markham fresh out of high school, and it hadn't been long before she was promoted to be his secretary. Over the years, he had reason to believe that the company had expanded to its present state in good part because of her expertise and loyalty.

"It seems Kirk asked her to call around to see if there were any vacancies in the motels."

"Why would he do that?"

"Temper, perhaps? If you remember he went off to his room rather suddenly after the, er, episode in the placito. You've got to admit that Charla looked a little stormy until she pulled herself together. Anyway, I told Della to tell him there weren't any rooms available. If you recall, an important part of our plan is to keep them under one roof."

"How did you explain why to her?"

"With Della you don't have to explain."

The last of the awards were given to the winners, and the band started playing. Charles and Tyson were both good dancers, but the women they'd escorted were off re-

53

pairing their makeup. They watched as several people at the next table rose to go to the dance floor.

Joe Letterman was one of the party, but he remained seated. He signaled the waiter to bring him another drink.

"What's with Joe?" Tyson asked, noting his surly expression.

"I guess it's because Charla turned him down when he went to get her."

Heavy eyebrows, black slashes like his son's, rose in question. "I thought you said she hadn't planned to come?"

"I guess I forgot to tell him that little detail when I suggested she might have changed her mind."

Tyson immediately recognized the mischief glinting in the eyes of his lifelong friend. It was much like the one that gleamed in his when they plotted one of their little escapades. "All right, tell me what you've been up to!"

The innocent look didn't deceive him. Charles knew it and broke into a grin. "You know how disgustingly platonic Charla keeps his dates. I noticed last night how, once I introduced Kirk to him, Joe was suddenly acting very possessive about her. When I saw him tonight, I thought it wouldn't hurt to stir things a little and mentioned Charla was home alone with Kirk."

Tyson chuckled, already on his friend's wavelength. "I'd have loved to be a fly on the wall. From his black looks, things were cooking at the ole hacienda!"

"A little jealousy never hurt anyone," Charles argued complacently. "I always say it acts as a leavening, helps bring events to a head."

"You should know. You always boasted it was a waste of energy—until you met Greta."

Charles's eyes grew soft with memories. Once he realized Greta was the woman he'd been waiting for, he had spent days agonizing whether she could return that love. Tyson had been invaluable in helping him eliminate the formidable competition. Jealousy? Oh, my, yes. He'd found out how it could tear at one.

"What do you think we should do next?" Tyson pressed his friend.

"Charla is giving signs of being a little gun-shy, so I suggest we back off for a while and let things settle down. I guess it's my fault for pushing all those men under her nose." He gave a heartfelt sigh. "I'll be glad when the wedding is over and we can wait for those grandchildren to come."

"Who do you think we should contact about the flowers for the wedding? Not to forget the caterer."

The two white heads bent together as they updated their war plan.

CHAPTER FIVE

Maria was more than the housekeeper; she had been part of the family since Charla's parents were married. To her, Charla and Kirk were the children she never had. She thought she was stern with them, but early on, they learned how soft her heart really was.

One of Kirk's favorite dishes had been her lamb stew, redolent with spices and thick rich gravy. When Maria set a plate of the succulent stew before him, his arm snaked out around her waist and he gave her a hug, much as he had as a youngster when begging for one of her outsize cookies that kept a growing boy from starving.

"Do you know I've stopped ordering it in restaurants," he told the giggling housekeeper. "I've been disappointed too often. No one can make it like you do. If I ever marry, you have to promise to give the recipe to my wife."

"Just like a man," Charla said sourly after the pleased woman returned to the kitchen. "Why your wife? Did it ever occur to you that kitchen work isn't necessarily the private domain of a woman?"

He arched a black brow at her. "You disappoint me, Charla. I thought you were an independent thinker and not brainwashed by what comes from the more strident woman libbers. Did your mother ever seem oppressed when she did something special to please your father? I know my mother didn't. Have you forgotten how our fathers returned that caring? To me, that sharing and giving is what love is all about. Believe me, if I ever find a woman like either of our mothers, my father can stop moaning over not having a grandchild to dangle on his knee."

"Good luck," she muttered, resenting the put-down but knowing his words held truth. She decided her best option was to change the topic of conversation.

"When we were talking before about the problem at the plant, I wasn't questioning how the rejected product was sent. I know how they're shipped. Dad's greatest concern is how they managed to get by the various inspections that he set up. The system sounded foolproof to me."

"When the human element is involved, nothing is foolproof. The fact that inferior parts did get shipped indicates someone has figured out a way to get past them."

"That's obvious. But how do you go about discovering how it's done?"

He smiled, remembering the same inquisitive look on her face when as a child she tried to follow what he happened to be involved in at the time. Some things never changed. He wondered fleetingly why that discovery gave him pleasure.

"There are different ways of working. My usual approach is to try to think like the person who's creating the problem—in this case, the person who's sending the damaged parts. What I would do if I were in that person's place. Usually, something emerges that clues me in on a lead I can follow."

"I think what bothers Dad the most is the fact that someone at the plant must be behind this. You know how proud he's been of their loyalty. They aren't just his employees. They're like family. He cares about them and is concerned when they are sick or have problems at home."

"It's apparent that there's at least one person at the plant who needs a refresher on loyalty," he said, referring to Joe Letterman.

She was concentrating on the food, and he watched for some reaction. He had made the inference to Letterman

57

purposely. For some reason it annoyed him how she was ignoring that incident in the foyer.

"What do you plan to do next?" she asked as he refilled their wine goblets.

"Spend more time at the plant tomorrow. Your father also wants me to check the inspection system for flaws and ways to improve it. He doesn't like the idea that anything even got as far as the packing house. I want to see the whole process and meet those working the machines."

Charla remembered the ponderous machinery, the connecting pulleys, and the peculiar humming sound they gave off. Then there were the presses that thumped as they stamped out a form on the shining sheets of steel. Each thump was a pulse beat that seemed to give life to the throbbing machinery. It had been a long time since she'd been beyond the office complex. It would be interesting to see what changes had been made.

For dessert, Maria brought in generous slices of strawberry rhubarb pie, another of Kirk's favorites. Charla poured coffee from the silver pot placed before her. When they were alone again, she shook her head in wonder. "The way she's catering to you, one would think you were the prodigal son returning," she remarked dryly.

Kirk tasted the first bite with pleasure before answering. "I think she's reminding me about my promise."

"Promise?"

"That I'd marry her when I grew up. She said she'd wait."

Charla snorted in derision. "You mean that's how you conned her into giving you those cookies all the time?"

He smiled as he took another bite. "At the time, I thought it was a good reason to offer marriage." Kirk looked directly at her. "Of course, since then I've discovered there are other reasons for forming relationships. But individuals approach them different ways. What approach is Joe using?"

Charla was taking a cautious sip of the hot coffee and

gulped in surprise, burning her mouth. She grabbed quickly for her ice water before exploding. "Who did you say?"

"Joe. You know, Joe Letterman, the man you were in a clinch with in the entrance hall." He watched her reaction with a carefully bland expression. He'd learned long ago that it was wise to case the territory before making his move—in business or pleasure. Her gorgeous blue eyes were storming and girding for battle.

"I don't indulge in 'clinches.' And if I did, they'd be no concern of yours!"

"But that's where you're wrong. I have to work with Letterman to get to the bottom of what's going on. He knows I'm staying here. If he's antagonistic, as I would be in his shoes, it will take me longer to solve the problem. I still have hopes of getting in some of the vacation I gave up to help your father."

"He has no reason to be antagonistic because of me," she replied stiffly. "We're no more than casual friends."

"Then tell me why he prances around like a rooster on a hot plate when he sees us together? He was fine when we were first introduced—until *you* came on the scene. In my book, that means he thinks he's being threatened. Just how casual is your casual?" He watched, enchanted, as her anger flared. She was breathtaking in her temper. She might not indulge in clinches, but he was struggling not to push back his chair and show her what clinches were all about.

Charla resented the picture he painted. She still hadn't figured out Joe's uncharacteristic behavior. "I don't want to discuss it. Either change the subject or you can finish dessert by yourself."

Kirk stilled his grin. Now she was being haughty, the princess quelling a subject who dared to step out of line. He loved it.

"Okay, though I don't know why you're acting so touchy. It was your father who said he expected wedding bells just before he introduced me to Letterman."

"What?" The fork clattered on the plate. "I don't believe he said that!"

"No?" he insinuated slyly. "It looks like Letterman has the required qualifications—college education, belongs to the right clubs. Why, your father even thought enough of the man to put him in charge of his beloved factory when he decided to give up the active running of it."

"Oh, no!" Her groan held disgust. "Here I thought it was safe to go out with him. I could feel comfortable with him because it seemed that he was one man Dad wasn't pushing."

Kirk's voice was properly sympathetic. "Simply a different tactic, my dear. Believe me, I recognize it from experience. Tyson has tried them all out on me."

"What's wrong with those old reprobates? Can't they leave us alone?"

Kirk was pleased to hear the plural that included him. It was a crack in the defensive wall she had erected, and he had every intention of widening it. And now that she was wary, Joe was eliminated as a contender. Nothing was more annoying than an eager matchmaking parent. He knew. There'd been several interesting women he had stopped seeing when he had realized his father was pulling strings behind the scene.

"Believe me, I know what you've been going through." His voice was sympathetic as they left the dining room, and his arm rested lightly across her shoulders. "Why do you think I set up my office in St. Louis even though I'd have preferred Santa Fe?" That should get more sympathy. His conscience barely quivered at the twisting of facts. One used any trick one could to achieve the desired results. Hadn't he had two of the best teachers?

"How can two otherwise wonderful people have such one-track minds!" she cried in outrage.

"You know why." He adroitly bypassed the chair she headed for and led her to the sofa.

60

"Yes. Grandchildren. I can't figure out why they've become so hepped on the subject."

"Because all their friends have them, and they feel left out. They can't match their bragging." He joined her close on the couch. Still incensed, she hadn't as yet become aware that he was caressing her hand.

"That's what they say, but of all the stupid reasons!" she steamed. "I threatened Dad that if he didn't stop, I'd adopt a child just to get him off my back. In fact, I'm seriously considering it. There's a lovely little boy on the reservation whose mother has died. I'd love to adopt him if I could only locate the father."

He looked at her in surprise. Yes, she would do it—and for love, not to stifle her father's matchmaking. "I don't think that would deter them."

"No, I guess not." She sighed, letting the last of the frustration seep from her. It was good to be able to talk to a man who understood what she had to put up with. The poor fellow was faced with the same problem.

She looked at him warmly, then stiffened. "What are you doing?"

Kirk looked up from the fingers he was kissing. "Your hands intrigue me. They're the hands of an artist, long and slender. They look fragile, but they have strength in them." He rubbed her palm along the hard curve of his jaw while staring into her startled eyes. "I've been wondering how they'd feel sliding over my skin. Soft and testing . . . or firm and searching?"

Her tongue moistened her suddenly dry lips. Charla knew it had been the wrong thing to do when his eyes shifted to take in their glistening outline.

"Ah, Charla!"

And like the night before, she was unable to protest or make the slightest move as his head slowly lowered. His pewter eyes could hold fire, flaming darts of hot desire that added to the heated warmth filling her body. Somehow he had managed to bring that warmth to life while she'd been busy exhorting her parent.

No, she had to admit honestly. The melting had started when she'd first stepped into the living room and saw Kirk. It was why she had been so incensed when Joe had kissed her. It had been the wrong man kissing her, she suddenly realized.

Lips firm yet soft, hot yet cool brushed hers as he tested and tasted. Then, as if satisfied that he would meet no resistance, his tongue slid into her mouth. It wasn't long before the small darting forays succeeded in whetting his appetite for further exploration. The sound rising in his throat held the exultation of the explorer knowing he had found a treasure far beyond his wildest dream.

The sound triggered a wildness in Charla. Her hands slid up his arms and across the width of his shoulders to his neck. The heat from his body was a burning message impossible to ignore. She arched in a need to add her fire to his. He shifted over her to accommodate her. The pressure eased infinitesimally on her mouth, causing her hands to plow through his thick crop of hair in a desperate need to prevent further retreat. Dear Lord, how could she have thought she knew what it was like to be kissed!

Kirk covered her mouth with his, responding to the urgency in her hands. Those hands! Ah, yes, there was strength in them as he'd anticipated. They kneaded trails of fire across his shoulders. But he wanted more, much more. He wanted them burning paths over his body, wanted them to know him as intimately as his own wanted to know her.

With quick impatience, the knit shirt was pulled off over his head. Charla's shirt followed before she could do more than gulp for air. Then she was back in his arms. He became slightly drunk from the sensation of her full soft breasts against his chest.

Then his hands taught her lessons on how efficient they'd become in augmenting the pleasure of kissing. Had the brat really wondered about that in that long-ago stolen kiss? God, her skin was a delight! Warm as the gentle kiss of the sun, smooth as the tantalizing silkiness of satin. He couldn't get enough of her. His mouth moved down her neck until it found the urgent peak that it coveted.

He drew it deep in his mouth, driven by her soft whimpering gasps of pleasure. Pleasuring her became his driving need because in her pleasure, he knew with a deep inner conviction that he himself would experience more than he ever had before.

A clattering noise rasped into his consciousness. Charla stiffened under him, and he lifted his head to listen. He ached with loss when the feverish exploration of her hands over his back stilled.

"Oh, my God, what are we doing? Maria will see us! She's cleaning off the table in the dining room."

Then her sweet hands were pushing him away. The door to the dining room was open, but they were stretched on the sofa with the high back acting as a shield.

"Shh. Be still," he soothed. "She can't see us." Her struggles stopped, but he knew from her tense posture that the mood was broken, beyond recapturing. His forehead dropped to her shoulder as he came to terms with his frustration.

He reached for their shirts and helped her into hers before slipping on his own. "Maybe it's just as well," he said ruefully as he brushed back a strand of long black hair that had escaped from her braid. "The sofa is not the place I'd choose for the first time we make love."

"Aren't you taking a lot for granted?" she questioned coolly. "I have no intention that there *will* be a first time."

Her haughty look was back, and he restrained a smile. Her protest lost something with lips crushed and rosy red from his kisses. "You can say what you want, honey, but we both know that in a few more minutes nothing short of an earthquake could have stopped us. Let's at least be honest with ourselves. You wanted it as much as I did. And

63

knowing that, can you truthfully say that you wish it hadn't ended differently? Believe me, there will be another time. We'll come together again with the same fire. Then not even that earthquake will be capable of stopping us."

He bent to place a quick hard kiss on her swollen lips and rose achingly to his feet. The cold shower he planned to take had better work or it was going to be a long night. He left the room, carrying with him the vision of a wide-eyed Charla, her fingers pressed to her lips. Did cold showers work for women?

CHAPTER SIX

Charla went through the living room on her way to breakfast. She stopped short when she saw the extra sofa pillows still strewn on the floor where they had been tossed the night before. Did the one they'd used still hold the imprint of their heads? She'd fluffed it guiltily before replacing the others. Had her father seen the disarray, guessed at the reason?

She searched his face while they ate, but he was busy reporting who won what at the tournament. She didn't like the depth of her sigh of relief.

Kirk, her father finally informed her, had already eaten and was at the plant. "I feel guilty taking him away from his vacation. But with any luck, he'll have everything solved in short order and can get in some time to do his thing. A man needs his R and R to recharge his batteries."

"His batteries don't need recharging," she muttered. She hadn't meant to say that and ducked her head in annoyance while buttering her toast. As a result she didn't see the gleeful look that sprang into her father's eyes.

"Do you have a golf date this morning?"

"It's been canceled. I thought I'd go to the plant and see if there's any way I can help Kirk with his investigation. The more information he has, the quicker he'll be through."

"Amen." She smiled apologetically when she saw his

exasperation. She had to do something about her loose tongue.

"I thought we discussed your attitude," he reprimanded her. "No one ever questioned the Treemont hospitality."

"Don't worry, Dad. No one ever will." But did that famed hospitality include enthusiastic response to mind-bending kisses on the sofa? The concept had her shifting the silver by her plate with nervous fingers.

"Last night I was remembering how Mom used to take me with her to the plant and how I enjoyed watching all the machinery running," she said as he placed his napkin on the table and rose to leave. "It's been a long time since I paid a visit. Have there been many changes?"

Charles smiled as he placed a kiss on her forehead. "Why don't you go and see? I'm certain Joe will be happy to give you a tour."

She grimaced. Joe! After his behavior the night before, she had no desire to see him again. "It was only a passing thought. I'll be too busy this week, anyway."

A short time later she was driving down the highway, sorting out what had to be done at the store. It was better than facing the reason behind her sudden desire to visit the plant.

Charla drove the van into town and decided it was in dire need of its weekly bath. After emerging from the car wash, she wondered, as usual, why she bothered. The layer of red dust would be back before the day was over after traveling rutted lanes to check if any of her suppliers had anything for the post.

Keeping it clean was a matter of pride, she admitted. The magnetic sign on the van advertised The Trading Post. It was her baby. She had conceived it, given it birth, and watched proudly as it took the first stumbling steps. It now walked with a jaunty stride, as indicated by the healthy ledger.

She understood why her father called her to task on the

Treemont hospitality. It was part of that pride he'd bred in her. But where had that pride been, allowing a guest to seduce her in her own living room?

Her hands tightened on the steering wheel. Allowed? She'd joined and abetted him. A dull ache started deep within her as she recalled how her hands had moved hungrily over his heated flesh, had kneaded and memorized with agonizing urgency the flat bands of muscles crossing his back. Her mouth had opened, willingly, hungrily to his urging. Their tongues had dueled in an erotic dance with an equal desire.

By the time she parked behind the store, her heart was pounding furiously in her chest. Charla was forced to sit for several minutes, drawing in deep breaths until the thunder stilled. There was a lesson here. If just remembering the passion he'd drawn from her could produce this reaction, she'd be smart to make certain they kept their distance. Kirk's stay could be counted in days, and she was not one to indulge in a quick affair.

But how could she have forgotten how he could always flip her emotions into high gear? Her memories of the vacations spent together were of seething frustrations or anger, of gusty laughter or hysterical tears. When Kirk was around, there never seemed to be a middle ground. Nothing had changed. With maturity, he'd simply learned how to stir a different set of emotions. And she'd be a fool to think it any more complicated than that.

Rosemary greeted her cheerfully when she entered the shop. She was her right hand, and as usual, Charla had to admire her dark handsome looks. She was a Navajo, tall and graceful, with aquiline features.

"It's a good thing you told me you wanted that painting of Mary's," she informed her. "Johnny was looking at it to decide about the frame when a customer tried to grab it from his hands. I had a hard time convincing him it was already sold. He ended up buying the one of her daughter holding the kachina doll."

"I better write that check so you can put the sold sign on it," Charla replied. She'd learned not to let the artists know if she intended to buy one of their works since they usually insisted on giving it to her in gratitude for what she was doing for them. She knew how important the money was to their livelihoods.

She examined the layout of the shop as Rosemary went over the report of the previous day. The rugs were moving slowly. Some were works of art, and she wished they had more room so they could be hung and shown to full advantage. The pottery, always a good seller, was doing well, as were the kachina dolls.

"Henry Mason's necklaces have become a hot item," Rosemary said in conclusion. "There was a woman in yesterday asking a lot of questions about him. I have a feeling she's a buyer for a chain of stores. This could be the break he needs to get into the big time."

"It couldn't happen to a more deserving person." Henry's youth had surprised her when he'd come to show her his silver jewelry. She'd made space for him immediately and had encouraged his natural ability. Maybe she should make a point to visit him, she thought. He was young, and if a buyer were interested in him, he would need advice on the importance of taking a contract to a lawyer before signing anything.

Charla went to help one of their saleswomen finish placing the pottery she had brought in the day before. Sally had the round face and squat body typical of the Hopi. Her pregnancy was advanced, but she had insisted on helping through this busy time. Charla had hired Sally after overhearing two of her sales crew talking about her deep longing for a new crib for this baby, her first. When Sally and her husband Peter Fallen were first married, Charla had learned that he had been out of work for a year and had talked Joe into giving him a job at the plant.

"Let me unpack them and hand them to you to place," Charla instructed. "How much longer do you have?"

The woman smiled serenely. "The doctor said a month, but my mother says it will come with the next moon."

"That's in two weeks. Is the nursery ready?"

"Oh, yes. Peter finished painting the room last week, and we bought the furniture."

"It's going to be a big healthy boy," she informed Sally, knowing that that was what she was praying for.

Sally ducked her head shyly. "I know. I went to Matia and she read the bones."

Charla laughed. "See! We can't both be wrong."

Matia, the local shaman, was an old woman who lived on the reservation in an equally old jacal. The simple house made of wood and mud was kept livable by grateful patrons of her ancient art. Her bag of dried bones were consulted before births and marriages and when any major problem needed resolving. Charla had thought nothing unusual in visiting her before starting the shop. It was in answer to her Indian heritage.

Charla could recall that visit in minute detail. The dim interior of the shack had been lighted by a small fire. She managed not to quiver under the long, hard stare from black button eyes that seemed to see into her soul. The shaman then rose arthritically from her ancient rocking chair to sprinkle a selection of herbs on the fire. The aroma had at first stung her nose and eyes before soothing her in an indescribably calming way. Matia had then untied the leather pouch from her waist and chanted with eyes closed before upending the contents on the table. Charla had watched in fascination as she bent over the assortment of small bones, touching each one lightly with the tip of one finger. It was as if that contact were a necessary adjunct to absorb all the message being disclosed for her eyes alone. The woman had then agreed that the venture would succeed in its intent and had given her additional names of various artisans to contact.

The bells fastened to the door jingled, pulling Charla's

attention back to the shop. She glanced over her shoulder and smiled widely as she went to greet the newcomers.

"Jane, how good to see you. Have you heard from Luis lately?"

The Indian woman came in slowly, her body heavy with child. "He sent card from California. He working lettuce field now. Next week it will be tomatoes."

"That's good to hear. Will he be able to be here when the baby comes?"

Her smile faded to be replaced with a stoic expression. "Maybe."

Charla wanted to kick herself. Of course he wouldn't. It cost too much and took time away from the important harvest season. After marrying the Mexican, Jane had gone with him to join the migrant workers. Her last pregnancy had been difficult and she'd lost the child, so they had decided that it was best if she remained behind this time with her people.

Charla smiled down at the small boy looking at her adoringly while clinging shyly to his aunt's skirt. "Hello, John. How's your tooth?"

He opened his mouth to show her the gap. The new tooth was already pushing into place. The baby tooth had refused to give way, and Charla had taken him to the dentist to have it extracted. After the small ordeal, she had brought him home for an ice cream treat. He'd become enchanted with the puppy they'd kept from the stable dog's litter. It was then that the near accident with Kirk's car had occurred.

"Are you going to take us on that picnic?" he asked eagerly.

"Sst!" Jane hushed, appalled by his question.

Charla laughed. "That's all right. I did promise to take him and his friends on one. It will have to wait until next week when we're not so busy." Her hand rested lovingly on the boy's silky dark hair. "Is that all right with you, John?"

His dark eyes gleamed happily, and Charla fought the urge to hug him. "If you go to Rosemary, I think she has some lollipops. And if I remember right, there's a red one."

He grinned widely, and she watched him race to the small office before turning to Jane. She was busy unwrapping a black cloth and separating the silver and turquoise necklaces for Charla's inspection.

"Have you heard from his father?" she asked casually while checking the quality of the workmanship. John's mother had been Jane's sister. The husband had disappeared after learning she was pregnant. One unconfirmed report was that he'd been seen in San Francisco, another in Oregon.

The woman's gutteral sound held disgust. "We'll never hear from Big John. A child would interfere with his freedom."

"If you want me to, I'll see what can be done about tracing him. He should help in the support of his son."

Pride brought the woman's head up. "We can take care of our own."

Careful, Charla warned. When she'd first seen the bright and inquisitive child, she'd fallen in love with him. He was the child she was eager to adopt. While the family was close to destitute, she knew only too well how strong and deep the family ties were. They'd relinquish their rights only if they thought it best for the boy. The size of her bank account would play no part in their decision.

"I was thinking mainly that it might prove wise to get him to sign a release. You never know, he might return someday in the future and decide to take his son away with him."

She fingered the jewelry, pretending to be unaware of the dark eyes examining her thoughtfully. "I'll take all but these two necklaces. Tell your brother he's being careless again. The fittings are loose. I warned him not to skimp on the size of the prongs. Remind him that his name goes

71

with the purchase. I'm sure he doesn't want to get the reputation for shoddy workmanship."

She gave the ones selected to Rosemary to price and list on the proper file card. She took John by the hand, leaving her assistant to tally up the money due from sales, minus commission, since the last time Jane had been in.

"Did you give the puppy a name?" John asked as he carefully unwrapped the paper from the red lollipop.

"I think they're calling him Racer. He races around all the time."

He tilted his head in an old wise look that Charla thought was adorable as he considered the choice. "He does run fast, doesn't he!" His expression turned anxious. "Bumping into the car didn't hurt him, did it?"

"No, it must have been a gentle bump," she assured him.

He grinned, displaying the gap in his mouth. "Boy, you told that man off! I bet he won't come around anymore!"

If that were only true! "His name is Kirk Webster, and he's staying at the house. He's an old friend of my family."

He sucked lustily on the lollipop while digesting the information. "My father is tall like him. I bet he drives the same kind of car, too."

Charla's throat tightened. He'd never seen his ne'er-do-well father. What kind of dreams was he substituting?

"But my father is better looking. He doesn't have all that white in his hair."

"I'm quite certain you're right," she managed. "Tell me, what shall I bring to drink on the picnic?"

"Chocolate milk!" he said instantly. Maria had introduced him to it that day, and he thought it was the most delicious drink going.

"Chocolate milk it will be."

"And chocolate chip cookies?" he added hopefully.

She recalled one visit when she'd given him a bag of chocolate candies. His face had held pure bliss as they were devoured. "You're a man after my own heart, John. Chocolate is my favorite, too."

Jane came down the aisle. Taking the boy's sticky hand, she thanked Charla before urging him from the shop.

Charla watched longingly as they climbed into an old rusty truck and drove away. John was too bright not to have the benefits of the education she could provide for him. If only there were a way she could adopt him! And in spite of Jane's reluctance, the first step was to find the missing father for that necessary release.

Her father should know how she should proceed. For the first time, she realized the subject had never been brought to his attention. Was it because she knew in her heart that there was little hope for success?

A faint heart never won a thing, she reminded herself briskly. Kirk came unbidden to her mind. Of course! With his background, he was just the man to tell her what her next move should be. She could hardly wait until the evening to ask him about it.

It was as good an excuse as any.

CHAPTER SEVEN

Kirk parked the Jaguar in a visitor's slot and looked grimly at the adobe-faced building. Treemont, Inc., was a small but important industry in a town that depended primarily on tourism for its survival. He could appreciate Charles's concern over retaining the lucrative government contract. When in full production, they had no more than one hundred people under hire. Even so, Santa Fe had few industries. The plant's collapse would hurt more than just those on the payroll.

He unlocked the glove compartment and pulled out the identification badge that Letterman had supplied and attached it to his shirt. The thought of the man brought a deepening frown to his face. Letterman had been very distant the day before. It was unfortunate that the man's antagonism leaked over from his private life, Kirk thought. Still, he couldn't blame him. He'd be the first one to bring out the dueling pistols if someone tried to intrude on what he considered his.

And he was the intruder. He usually respected the hands-off signs, but Charla had stirred something deep and unsettling in him, something he felt driven to examine more fully. He'd like to reassure Joe that he had nothing to worry about, that he'd be gone as soon as the culprit was discovered. After all, he still had that vacation time due him. But the excitement Charla stirred in him might not be resolved by then. And he was never a man to leave a problem—or challenge—unresolved.

Kirk stepped out of the car and locked it. The guard at the gate greeted him as he started toward the plant. He noticed with satisfaction that the man's apparent friendliness didn't stop him from checking the badge and making him sign in as per orders.

"Do all visitors have to sign in?" he asked as he wrote his name in the log book.

"Definitely, as well as all office personnel. In and out. Those working in the plant go through the back entrance where they have to punch the time clock."

"Is a guard stationed there also?"

"Yes. His job is to check that they punch only their own card."

Kirk had been told the routine down to the last detail. Security was so tight that when leaving, lunch boxes had to be opened for inspection as well as any bags they carried. Some of the parts manufactured were for highly secret projects.

"Sir?"

Kirk stopped at the guard's tentative question. "You have something to add?"

"Just that we all hope you find out who's behind this. Mr. Treemont has been a wonderful boss, and we're upset that anyone could do this to him."

Kirk took in the man's intense look. It was obvious that his sense of loyalty was outraged that one of them was doing something to threaten the reputation of the man they admired. "I'll do my best. Just keep your eyes and ears open. If you hear anything the least bit suspect, let me know. Sometimes it's the little pieces that are most important."

The man's chin lifted with determination. "I'll put the word out and see that anything suspicious gets back to you."

Kirk thanked him, wincing at visions of being inundated

by all sorts of unrelated trash that he'd have to wade through. But what he'd said held true. More than once it had been the small, obscure piece of gossip that had given him the lead that solved a difficult case.

The sun was promising another hot day, and he stepped gratefully into the air-conditioned building. The receptionist waved abnormally long fingernails at him and pouted with perfectly outlined lips. He winked in acknowledgment of the little seduction act and started down the hall to the small office Joe had provided for his use.

"Mr. Letterman would like you to stop in to see him," she purred.

She pressed the button on the intercom before Kirk could stop her and made her announcement. He didn't particularly want to see Letterman until he had something to report. After last night's encounter, he was certain the atmosphere between them would be even more strained.

It was. Brown eyes stared at him frostily across the desk when he entered the office. Letterman didn't rise or offer a hand as he'd done the day before.

"Thank you for stopping by," he said curtly. "I wanted to see you before you went into the plant today."

Kirk raised a black eyebrow as he settled into a leather chair. Although it hadn't been offered, he might as well be comfortable while Letterman unloaded his spleen.

"You *do* know that some of the parts we manufacture here are highly secret."

Kirk didn't bother to acknowledge the statement. The fact had been given to him the day before. Besides, that was why he had been called in.

"I know Charles said you're to have freedom of the plant, but I want to impress on you that some places are off limits."

Anger stirred. So he wanted to flex his muscles, did he?

"I'm assigning one of my men to accompany you. He'll be able to screen answers to any questions you might have in those areas."

"Mr. Treemont knows that I don't work under restrictions," Kirk returned coolly. "He guaranteed that I would have complete freedom." He didn't like pulling rank on the man, but his job was difficult enough without unnecessary barriers being erected.

A dusky flush colored Joe's cheeks. "I'm supervisor of this plant and as such have been given full responsibility for what goes on in it. My decision stands. Of course, if you can't work within that framework, you're free to complain to Mr. Treemont."

Kirk forced his body to remain relaxed. He wasn't about to let Letterman see he recognized the challenge as the insult it was. Did the snit expect him to run to Charles and cry for help?

They both knew that the plant's safety was not behind this flaunting of authority. The man was using the inconvenience as a way to get back at him. He evidently equated Charla's rejection the night before with Kirk's being at the house.

"We'll see how it works," Kirk temporized. He rose to leave before the polite veneer tore and words were exchanged that they'd both regret.

Joe knew better than to let the smile of success show. "I'll send Harvey Stone to your office. He's been with us for years and knows the plant well. By the way, I expect a daily report on your progress."

Kirk stopped in midstride and turned to immobilize the man behind the desk with stabbing gray eyes. "There seems to be a misunderstanding. I report directly to Mr. Treemont. If there's anything I think you need to know, you'll get it verbally. A typed final report is given when the case is resolved. It will be up to Mr. Treemont how much of it he wishes to share with anyone else."

Joe stared at the closed door for several minutes before moving. He'd pushed hard before, but he'd never encountered this feeling of intense danger. For several heartbeats, he'd relived a fear similar to the time he'd come upon a seven-foot rattlesnake.

Harvey Stone, while inoffensive in himself, was the worst possible shadow that Kirk could have. He was one of the assistant supervisors and as such was part of the hierarchy in the front office. Kirk was proud of the way he could get the most reluctant person to open up to him. With Harvey at his shoulder, there was no way those he questioned would return more than guarded monosyllables.

He was thoroughly frustrated by the time the shift was ready to quit. He had no desire to give Letterman the satisfaction of complaining to Charles, but if he didn't get Harvey off his back, he might as well give up. The thought grated, adding to his irritation.

"Do you plan to stay to check the next shift?" Harvey asked when Kirk made no move to leave.

"Yes, but there's no need for you to remain," Kirk answered with a sigh of relief. Maybe now he'd get something done.

"I was just checking. Joe said I should let him know if you do so he can assign someone else to take my place."

Kirk's jaw tensed as he clamped down on the words boiling to come out. It wouldn't solve anything to demolish Harvey. He was just an innocent puppet in this game Letterman was playing.

He stalked away to the packing end of the plant. Things were in a mess. What the hell did Letterman think he could accomplish with these blocks he was putting in the way? Kirk usually worked with some cloak of secrecy, but from the guard's offer to assist, it was obvious that the word was out on why he was there. Whoever was involved now had plenty of warning to cover his tracks. It would take an act of God to unearth any clues.

He watched with careful attention as the conveyor belt carried shiny metal parts to the packing table. With practiced efficiency they were nestled securely in the fitted cardboard boxes. Nimble fingers closed the tabs and put dampened tape across the lid, sealing it tight. A rubber stamp labeled it, and the finished product was stacked to be taken to the warehouse. There they were stored until needed to fill an order.

It was a common enough routine. He'd already investigated the various stations where the inspectors checked the finished parts, first visually, then by passing them under an X-ray machine to show if there were any inner cracks or blemishes. He'd seen only one rejection while watching. He knew Charles always insisted upon the best in his materials and equipment. And from his men. Yet somehow a less-than-best person had managed to get by and was creating havoc.

Though on the case only a short time, Kirk was no closer to solving the how and who and where. And if Letterman had his way, he'd be no further along at the end of the week.

Letterman. A frown furrowed between his eyes. Was Kirk blinding himself by assuming Charla was the reason for the man's antagonism? Could it be there was another reason why he was throwing up blocks to impede Kirk? His eyes hardened as the concept expanded. It wouldn't be the first time the culprit was the one least suspected. But Letterman had a top job at the plant. Losing the government contract could well cost him his position.

Kirk walked to the warehouse area and wandered through the lines of metal racks where the filled boxes were stored. A noise arrested his attention when he reached the far corner where the flat boxes were stacked. It came again, a long sawing sound. He was acclimated to the pulsing noise of the running machinery, but this had a foreign sound. He hesitated until he was certain it came from the direction of the boxes. A few steps brought him closer, permitting him to peer over the top.

A hollow space had been made behind the cardboard

wall of boxes. In the nest, a man was sound asleep, snoring with unconcerned abandonment. Kirk smiled grimly at the picture he made until he saw the wine bottle lying by the man's hand.

This wasn't a worker getting in a few minutes of rest. From the low level of the liquid in the bottle, he was sleeping off a drunk. Good God, was this how the defective parts had been substituted? How simple to slip a bottle to an Indian with their well-known low tolerance to liquor. It would then be simple to make the switch with one of the already sealed boxes while he was sleeping it off.

The anger and frustration had been bottled too long. With a searing oath, Kirk pushed aside a pack of boxes. Reaching with both hands, he clutched the shirt front and yanked the man from his cardboard bed. He sagged dazedly against Kirk and was slammed against the wall to keep him upright.

"Wha—what are you doing?" he asked feebly.

"Never mind what I'm doing," Kirk blazed. "I want some answers."

"First, I'd like to hear what your answer is to Pete's question."

Kirk's head snapped around. Charla stood there, fury blazing in her incredible blue eyes.

"Or is it your habit to bang a person's head against the wall and concuss him? Look at the poor man. He can't even focus his eyes. Does Dad know the Gestapo methods you use to try to get your information?"

Kirk's lip curled in a snarl. Enough was enough. He didn't need her sass added to the day's frustration. "Stay out of this, Charla. You don't know what you're talking about."

"Are you calling me stupid?" she seethed. "I have the evidence of my own eyes. What's with you? Is this how you get your kicks, beating on him because he's an Indian?"

That hurt. Those on Kirk's payroll were an admixture

of races and creeds. He hired people for their ability. It never occurred to him to select a person because of the color of their skin.

"Tell me, does your father approve of those in his employ sleeping on the job?" he asked in a low roar.

Charla blinked, momentarily disconcerted. She hadn't seen that part of it. She'd come upon them when Pete had been slammed against the wall. "If he was, it was because he's exhausted. His wife is expecting their first baby any minute."

Kirk released his grip, letting the man sag uncertainly against the wall. "Then we're lucky that he didn't ask everyone in the plant to celebrate the imminent arrival. They could have ordered a case of wine and had one big sleep-in."

Charla managed not to flinch under the force of anger he turned on her. "What are you talking about?"

Kirk reached into the walled-off nest to retrieve the bottle. "This," he grated, thrusting the bottle into her hands. "It's usually forbidden to drink on the job. In any place that I've ever worked, it would mean he'd be out on his can. Or does your sweet Letterman protect his own and turn a blind eye on such incidents?"

He didn't wait for an answer. He was too close to committing mayhem, too steaming mad to trust further talk. He strode away with long angry steps, not stopping until he was in his car. The wheels screamed an angry protest as he spun out of the parking lot.

It wasn't until he sliced by two cars and saw the frightened faces that he checked his speedometer. One hundred miles an hour was definitely above the speed limit, and he eased his foot from the floored accelerator.

Yet the wild ride had accomplished one thing: he was once again in control of his emotions. What was the matter with him, permitting Letterman to get to him like that? Where was his celebrated cool? Kirk wasn't happy with the way he'd handled the drunken man, but, dammit, did

Charla have to come at him like she had before finding out the facts?

That, he had to admit reluctantly, was the crux of his problem. He'd been frustrated long before the meeting with Letterman. Just looking at that enchanting woman made him ache. And after that episode on the sofa, he had gone beyond aching. He was in physical pain.

The road widened for a cross street, and he slowed to turn around and head back to Santa Fe. What was he going to do about her? After savoring the incredible softness of her skin, tasting the ambrosia hidden in her mouth, there was no other course open to him but to make her his. She was a sorceress, arousing him to an acute state of hunger. He had an uncomfortable conviction that only by satisfying that incredible need would he become free.

Which meant that as much as he'd like to renege on his commitment to help Charles and get out of the squeeze Letterman had him locked in, he had to return.

He smiled thinly recalling Charla's defiance. Lord, she was magnificent when her incredible eyes blazed with fury. She was like a goddess shooting down mere mortals with stormy thunderbolts. She'd stood glaring at him in defiance, her shoulders thrown back, thrusting her breasts forward under the thin cotton shirt.

His grip tightened on the steering wheel as he was seared with the memory of their soft fullness cupped in his hands. An excitement feathered his loins. The night before, she had unleashed a passion that had rocked him back on his heels. A man would be a damn fool not to accept the challenge and try for a repeat.

CHAPTER EIGHT

Charla glared scornfully at Kirk's retreating back. Just like a man, running off before she'd finished telling him what she thought of his actions. She knew she was hypersensitive where her Indian friends were concerned, but she was sick and tired of the treatment they were frequently subjected to as if they were second-class citizens. She still felt ill from the shock of discovering that her old playmate was one of the offenders.

"I feel awful." Pete's groan brought her attention back to him as he leaned weakly against the wall for support.

He looked ghastly. And well he should if he had consumed all that wine. She hated to admit it, but Kirk was right. Pete would be fired if the foreman discovered he was drinking on the job. Her main concern was for Sally, his wife, and the baby. There must be some way she could cover up his indiscretion. It wouldn't help flaying him with words while he was in his present condition. But once he was sober . . .

Footsteps echoed not far away in the cavernous warehouse. Peering through the grid made by the shelves, she caught a glimpse of Larry Perkins, the foreman of the section. If he saw Pete in such a state, there would be no way she could help Pete keep his job.

The incriminating evidence that Kirk had thrust at her with such disdain was hurriedly shoved in her shoulder bag. With luck, she might be able to get Pete out of the building before he was spotted.

"Let's get out of here. What you need is fresh air," she muttered. Grabbing his arm, she half led, half dragged him to the door. Not for the first time, she was thankful that she was tall and kept herself in shape. While shorter, Pete was heavyset. It took all her strength to guide his dragging steps as he sagged heavily against her for support.

The guard hurried to assist her when they reached the door. "He looks like hell. Should I send him to the infirmary?"

"I don't think it's necessary," Charla said quickly. "I think it's the bug that's going around. I'll take him home and let his wife nurse him."

The guard's look was doubtful. "You shouldn't do that. You'll catch it from him."

"I've already had it," she lied, desperate to get out of the place before Larry Perkins saw them. "Will you punch out his card?"

"Sure," he agreed, still not happy but bowing to the authority inherent in the Treemont name. "I'll tell the guys he shares a ride with what has happened. Do you know what pueblo he comes from?"

"Yes. His wife works in my store."

He nodded. They all respected what she was doing for the local Indians. "Sit him here. I'll watch him while you get your car."

They propped the limp man in the chair. Charla paused to assure the guard that she'd be right back and hurried around to the front of the building where her car was parked.

How did she get involved in these situations? she wondered in dismay. If she hadn't succumbed to her desire to see the plant again, she'd never have run into Kirk and been left to clean up after him. There was something wrong with her reasoning, but she was too upset to delve into it further.

When she'd arrived earlier at the plant, the receptionist had asked coyly if she wished to see Joe. Seeing him was the last thing she wanted, and she'd felt a fool assuring the woman that her intention was simply to visit the plant. The sickening coyness became knowing as the information was extended that Kirk Webster was touring the plant also, accompanied by Mr. Stone.

She ran into Harvey Stone a short time later. Charla had known the assistant supervisor since she had been a child. He'd been the source of candy drops on those long-ago visits. He explained to her teasingly that his coddling was over for the day, thank goodness, and that he was reporting in so the night super could continue on the next shift. Mr. Webster? Why, yes, she no doubt would run into him. He left him somewhere back by the warehouse section.

She didn't give Mr. Stone's odd choice of words further thought. Her interest was in seeing what improvements had been made at the plant, right? Then why was she practically making a beeline for the warehouse section? Fortunately, she never had time to answer the questions. Hearing Kirk's voice in the back of the storeroom, she'd hurried to surprise him. Only she was the one surprised when she saw him haul the befuddled Pete against the wall. Maybe she shouldn't have attacked him with such anger. For some ungodly reason, he seemed to trigger that emotion with effortless ease.

Charla reached the car and sighed while unlocking it. It went against the grain to admit he rated an apology. She had known it as soon as he'd thrust the bottle at her. However, if he hadn't been such a coward and run, he'd have been there to help her rescue Pete.

She frowned while steering the van to the back gate. Why was she so certain that he'd have gone along with this wild scheme to help Pete? Was it because as children they had matched wits so effortlessly and collaborated with such enthusiasm over their endless pranks?

The guard helped Pete into the van and she drove away

with a sigh of relief. She really hadn't expected to be able to pull it off. Pete groaned when she drove over a bump. Thinking of the distress Sally would experience over this, Charla had little sympathy for his discomfort. He was going to have the granddaddy of hangovers, and just maybe he'd be more circumspect the next time temptation came his way.

She stopped at a red light and spared a look at her passenger. He was sagging against the door as if he had been drugged. For the first time, she felt concern. Was he on drugs? Like elsewhere, it was becoming an increasing problem on the reservations. But, no, the bottle in her pocketbook was evidence enough of his problem.

Lost in her thoughts, she almost missed the turnoff to his pueblo. Considering how close Sally was to term, she hated bringing Pete to her in this condition. But Charla knew Sally would deal with it. She had seen stoic expressions on their faces often enough. It was how these Indian sisters of hers seemed to meet all problems.

Charla checked her image in the mirror and made a final adjustment to the skirt. The desired effect was achieved. Cool, detached, even regal. Her long black hair was braided in a coronet that sat like a crown on her head. Against the white silk-textured dress, her jewelry was striking. Heavy silver turquoise earrings hung from her lobes. They and the matching necklace and exquisite ring she wore had been a gift on her last birthday from all those involved in The Trading Post.

She usually didn't dress so carefully for a family dinner, but she felt the need to make a statement. With her stubborn pride, it wasn't going to be easy apologizing to Kirk. For some reason, she was in need of all the armament she could get.

Her father's mellow voice flowed out to her as she crossed the courtyard to the living room. She didn't like the way her body immediately tensed. Unless he'd brought home a guest, Kirk must already be there. Having made up her mind that he deserved an apology, she wanted to get it over with. It would only become more difficult the longer she delayed. If she gave it with her father there, it would mean having to explain Pete's part. Although Charles was benevolent where his employees were concerned, drinking on the job was one infraction he never tolerated. That would mean all her hectic manipulating would have been for nothing.

The two men had chosen comfortable chairs opposite each other. Charla paused in the doorway to examine Kirk's angular profile. His was an aggressive chin if she ever saw one. His firm mouth augmented the impression, increasing the warning. Unfortunately, the assessment had lost its impact. She had intimate knowledge of what a mind-blowing erotic tool his mouth could become.

Kirk's hand paused in bringing the glass he was holding to his lips. Did he sense her there, staring like some demented adolescent? Her gaze hurriedly shifted and met her father's alert eyes. Exasperation filled her expelled sigh. She knew all too well what his interpretation would be if he had caught her unguarded expression.

"There you are, my dear," Charles greeted her. "It must have been a hard day. You look like you need one of Kirk's excellent martinis."

"I believe I will. If you give your unqualified endorsement, they must be good."

Although she preferred not to sit on that particular sofa, she chose it because it was the farthest from Kirk. She saw it was a tactical mistake when after handing her the drink he joined her at the opposite end. It was impossible that his body heat could radiate that distance, she said firmly, and focused on her father.

"I hear you went to the plant, after all," he said with a pleased expression. "I ran into Harvey Stone and he told me. You should have stopped in to see Joe. He was upset to hear you'd been there without letting him know. He would have loved to show you all the new improvements we've been making."

Charla looked at him warily over her drink. What was he up to, dragging Joe into the conversation?

"I only had a limited amount of time to spend there. If he'd known, he'd have felt obligated to make a big production of it."

"Guess you're right. Did you run into Kirk? Were you still there, son?"

Charla looked at Kirk. How much of their disastrous meeting had he already told? He returned her look, but his long lashes hid any message.

"We met briefly," he said neutrally. "I was checking the warehouse section and left."

Charles hid his annoyance. Those lines of shelves filled with merchandise offered a fair amount of privacy. Had they really not taken advantage of the opportunities it presented? What was it with this younger generation?

"Did you come up with any new information today?"

Kirk took a sip of his drink before answering. "Nothing definite, but then I didn't expect to. What I'm checking are the more obvious ways the rejected parts could have slipped by the inspectors and gotten mailed. I know it's a special component made to government specifications, but how many companies do you send it to?"

"Four that I know of, but you should check with Joe Letterman."

"Did all four companies get imperfect parts?"

"No, two were sent to Sunco, and Intermac got one."

"What time span are we talking about?"

"The first complaint was filed six weeks ago. The last one came in ten days ago. I brought what was happening up to the board. We decided it would be wise to get on top of what was going on in a hurry. That's when you were contacted. The government contract comes up for renewal in three months. Needless to say, it will hurt us badly if we lose it. A lot of extra machinery has been bought on the strength of it. The payments are pretty heavy. Meeting them could be disastrous if the contract is given to a competitor."

Kirk digested the information for a brief minute. "Can you get me a list of who's been hired the last six months?"

Charles's mouth thinned. "I'll have Joe get it for you. So you think it's someone at the plant?"

A black eyebrow arched. "You have some other suggestion?"

Charles shook his head despondently. "I'm afraid not. I'd be a fool to hang on to the hope it was because our inspections were inadequate."

"That could be likely if it were an isolated case. But there have been too many in too short a time. Somebody wants to make sure the government is well aware of what's happening."

"I thank God that the imperfect parts were discovered so soon. The components are vital to the more advanced airplanes and rockets. I could never live with the thought that a death resulted from a malfunctioning part made by my company."

Charles looked gray, and Kirk rose to refill his glass. So much for Charla's foolish assertion that Charles and Tyson were plotting to get them together. She almost had him believing her wild assertions. If anything further developed between them it was because it was what they wanted.

What did he mean by "if"? *When* was the going word. True, they had explosive flare-ups, but they were like a fine spice. It added zest to whatever had started between them. There was no doubt in his mind that he wanted her—and in the not-too-distant future. He was adept at reading body language. He was satisfied that what he was reading was that this black-haired sorceress was in full accord.

Her subtle perfume enveloped him the moment he rejoined her on the sofa. It activated all-too-vivid memories of the sensations that had ripped through him when he'd taken her in his arms. He damned his susceptibility even as it brought to mind the way her breasts felt crushed against his chest, the sweetness of her soft lips parting to give access to the hidden ambrosia. It took a giant effort to smother the resultant reaction and concentrate on his discussion with Charles.

It was while they were waiting for dessert that Harvey Stone's name was again brought into the conversation. It triggered the question Charla had wanted to ask earlier in the day.

"Harvey sounded like he was baby-sitting you," she mocked. "He mentioned he'd spent the whole day tagging after you." That had stung, she noticed with a perverse satisfaction when the muscle along his jaw tensed. "What were you doing that needed coddling? I'm sure he'd have preferred to put in a more productive day."

"I'm certain he thought so, too," Kirk returned tersely. "Unfortunately, Letterman thinks otherwise."

Charles looked up in surprise. "Joe gave the order? Whatever for?"

"He's being careful that I don't stumble onto whatever secret projects you're involved in."

"But that's asinine! I told him that your past work gave you top clearance. Besides, your integrity was never under question."

Cold pewter eyes surveyed them both, revealing his irritation. "He seems to have forgotten it then."

Charles looked at him astutely, sensing the anger and frustration brought on by Joe's unwarranted action. "Did Harvey's presence interfere with your investigation?"

Kirk made no effort to disguise his bitterness. "Let's say that being tailed by someone from the front office didn't encourage anyone to open up when I questioned them."

Maria brought in the dessert. Nothing more was said as they gave their full appreciation to the strawberry mousse. But Kirk was satisfied. The expression on his host's face assured him that there would be no further road blocks put in his way as far as his investigation was concerned.

But what about Letterman's relationship with Charla? He glanced at the disturbing woman. He wasn't quite sure what had been between the two. Whatever, he was certain after Charla's negative response to Letterman's kiss that it was over. He had every intention to keep it that way.

The question was, how was he going to succeed? He hadn't been immune to the barb Charla sent him regarding her conversation with Harvey. It was evident she was still seething over the way he had handled that idiot he caught sleeping off a drunk. Did she really think he was going to report him? That wasn't his job unless it had something to do with how the substitution was effected.

When they returned to the living room, Charles excused himself, saying he had work waiting for him in the den. He was on several community committees, including setting up for the next tournament at the golf club, so it sounded logical. Charla, however, saw his defection as an excuse to leave them together. She was having no part in it and rose to leave.

"I have a lot to do also, what with the extra work this week at The Trading Post."

"Running, Charla?"

She met Kirk's teasing accusation defiantly. "What in the world would I be running from?"

"I don't know. You tell me."

She sent him a scathing look before turning to leave. She hesitated when she reached the door, recalling the promise she made to herself to get the apology over with before it became too difficult to give. His snide remarks weren't making it easy.

"I meant to apologize before," she said stiffly, keeping her back to him.

"That's nice, but apologize for what?"

"Accusing you as I did about Pete Fallen. I didn't know he'd been drinking."

"And I apologize for leaving you with him. Did he manage to snap out of it?"

91

"Not really. He looked so sick that I thought it best to get him home to his wife. Sally is one of my helpers at The Trading Post."

He frowned in concern. "But he could hardly walk. How did you manage?"

Intent on her story, Charla wasn't aware of returning to the sofa. She told him about hearing Larry Perkins coming and, because of concern for Sally, her need to get Pete out before he collapsed.

When she told how she got the unsuspecting guard to help her, he started chuckling. She joined him, recalling how she knew he'd appreciate her fancy footwork. It was good laughing again as they had when they'd shared audacious escapades.

"I never saw anyone out of it like he was. It was as if he were drugged. I had to help poor Sally get him to bed. She was in no condition to get him there by herself. I hope he doesn't miss too much time at work. With the baby coming any day, they can't afford to lose any of his salary."

"In cases like this, some companies send the paycheck home to the wife so the husband doesn't get his hands on it and spend it at the first tavern he gets to."

"That's the odd part. Pete has no history of drinking. His father was a hopeless case, and he vowed he'd never end that way."

"Then he better review his vow."

"I hope so, for Sally and the baby's sakes."

"Don't get too wound in their affairs, honey. They won't appreciate it."

His breath teased her cheek, and she looked up in surprise. When did they shift this close?

"I try not to," she managed in a whisper. In the subdued light, his eyes reminded her of the shining black agate known as Apache Tears. She could see her reflection in them. His lashes lowered, and she knew his gaze was fastened on her mouth. Recognizing the hunger, her heart gave a painful lurch before pounding at an accelerated rate. Such intense hunger couldn't go unanswered.

Her lips were already parted to accept the first brush of his tantalizing kiss. His mouth moved on to space light kisses along her cheeks, her eyes, her throat. They were delightful, but they didn't satisfy her own hunger.

The craving rose from deep within her, full blown, an aching need to be fed. She finally cupped his jaw to stop his exploring. It was her mouth that needed the replenishing only his could supply.

Her soft murmurs told of her frustrated desire. He recognized the call and was momentarily stunned by his surge of exultation. In answer his mouth found and settled over hers. He adjusted the fit and drank deeply of her sweetness. Had a woman ever tasted this heavenly, felt so perfect in his arms? Would he ever get enough of her? he wondered, and plundered further to possess all she offered. He was shaken by the overwhelming need to have this woman accept him, to accept that from this day on there could be no other.

There was something dangerous about this sofa. They were again stretched on it, their bodies straining in desperate need for each other. She pulled his shirt free so her hands could move avidly over his back. He found the edge of her dress, and his hand reveled in the enticement of the soft flesh of her inner thigh. He'd always been assured of his control, but what this woman did to him made such a claim useless.

Out of necessity his alert system had become finely honed over the years. Its efficiency was the only reason why the sound of approaching footsteps managed to penetrate the daze he was lost in.

He raised his head to see that Charles had left his den and was using the outside covered walk to go to the kitchen.

"Is something wrong, Kirk?" Please don't stop, every

pulsing nerve in her body begged. He was lying partially over her, pressing her into the soft cushions.

The question brought his gaze down to her. He was lost immediately in her fascinating eyes. He'd been enchanted when they sparked with anger, but seeing them sultry with passion was almost his undoing.

"Your father," he managed to answer. "It seems he's going for another serving of that strawberry mousse."

She blinked twice and stiffened. "Oh, my God, let me up!"

The mood was shattered in a repeat of the night before when Maria had intruded. He released her slowly, wondering if the pain incapacitating him would permit him to even sit up.

He swore fluently under his breath. Damn all chaperons. He had to get her away from this house, away from intruding situations. And he had to do it soon, before he went up in smoke.

CHAPTER NINE

Charles lined up his driver with the ball and swung with less than his usual enthusiasm. The ball took flight down the fairway, then hooked with its usual determination and flew into the rough.

Tyson looked at his friend quizzically. Something he saw in his face made him hold back a deserved caustic comment. Charles was practically handing him the game, something unheard of.

He waited until the game was over and their golf cart was left at the pro shop. "What's the matter, Charles? From the way you played I'd guess you're either coming down with a bug or had a rough night. I hate to think that age is finally catching up with you!"

Charles shot him a withering look as they went to the dining room. "You just wish!"

"If it's none of the above, what's eating at you? You've never made it this easy for me to win a free lunch."

Charles waited until the waiter took their order. "I've been thinking. Maybe we should forget about our war plan with the kids."

Tyson choked on the water he was drinking. "I don't believe what I'm hearing," he finally managed to gasp. "What brought on *that* crazy idea?"

His friend shifted uncomfortably in the chair. "It occurred to me that we have no right trying to manipulate them just because we think they're right for each other. If they're happy with their lives, who are we to try to change them?"

Black brows lowered in suspicion. "And what brought on that noble thought?"

Charles applied mustard to his Reuben sandwich before replying. "I'm thinking of Charla's welfare. She's totally immersed in The Trading Post. And you know how she's involved in the families at the different pueblos. It will hurt her to have to give that up. Besides, you must admit she makes a marvelous hostess at my parties."

Tyson gave an undignified snort. "So that's it! How selfish can you get, Charles Treemont! I never thought you so small as to think of your own comfort over your daughter's happiness. If it's a hostess you want, I don't have to remind you that there are dozens of unattached women out there who'd be willing to fill the post."

Charles bit defensively into his sandwich. His friend always had an irritating ability to get to the meat of the discussion.

Tyson watched placidly as his friend squirmed. "Now that we've got that settled, suppose you tell me just what happened."

"You should have seen them on the sofa last night!" He had stopped in shock when walking in on that hot scene. Hot? It was a good thing there had been no fire in the hearth. The room was ready to go up in flames from the outfall. In that instant, he had been forced to accept the fact that his daughter was a twenty-eight-year-old woman and not the little girl he carried close to his heart.

"You mean my boy has inherited the old Webster chemistry and all is alive and well!" Tyson exclaimed gleefully.

Charles glared at him. "He better put a harness on it. I won't have him stir up my girl unless he means something by it!"

Tyson's eyes lighted with devilish delight. "Oh, I dare say he meant something by it, all right. But you know, you just gave me an idea."

96

"I have one of my own. I'll send him packing home to you."

"Don't get carried away, pal. Remember those grandchildren we're working for. Now that we've got the old chemistry going, we have to see about keeping it in high gear. Think back when we were young. What kept us zeroing in on a particular woman?"

A reluctant smile softened Charles's repressive expression. As happened so often, he was latching on to Tyson's thought process. "The challenge of the chase."

"Amen," Tyson said fervently.

Charles's smile broadened. "Are you saying we should consider placing obstacles in their path?"

"Got it in one, pal!"

"How do we go about that? Remember, Kirk hopes to solve the problem at the plant quickly so he can get on with that vacation we pulled him from."

"If we work this right, he could well decide that Santa Fe is the best place for his vacation," Tyson said slyly.

"A few more kisses like they were exchanging on that sofa and he won't be in any condition to concentrate on solving the plant's problem," Charles muttered darkly.

"Good! The hotter the better," Tyson said, blithely dismissing any mental or health problems his son might suffer in the process.

The two men considered various adjustments to update their war plan. When they left the restaurant, Tyson pulled out a small white pad and flipped open to one of the pages.

"I figured white is for weddings," he said in answer to Charles's unspoken question. "You know how loose papers get lost, so I picked this up at the stationery store. I thought I'd give you an update on the caterers I've contacted."

Charles's eyes twinkled as he pulled out a similar pad. "Excellent! And I've checked on several florists to get an idea of what flowers are in season."

"That's the spirit, Charles," Tyson said, slapping his friend on the shoulder.

The two men happily compared notes as they walked to their cars. "By the way," Charles said, turning to the last page in the pad. "I've been thinking about a name for the first grandson. What do you think of 'David'?"

Tyson repeated the name thoughtfully. " 'David Webster.' Not bad. 'David Tyson Webster.' That has a good strong sound to it."

Charles nearly choked. "I was thinking more on the line of 'David Charles,' " he said stiffly.

Tyson smothered the laugh before he insulted his friend. "They don't have the same fit. Let's give it some more thought. After all, they're bound to want more than one child."

Charles perked up at the thought. "You know, I wouldn't mind a granddaughter. Can't you see a little Greta?"

They parted at their cars. Each drove home testing a variety of names for the grandchildren that were to be theirs in the not-too-distant future.

CHAPTER TEN

Rosemary looked up from the receipts they were going over in the tiny office and faintly whistled between her teeth. "Now *that's* what I call a hunk. Excuse me while I beat the others to take care of his wants. If I'm so lucky!" she tacked on with a lecherous grin.

Charla glanced over her shoulder. The door was open and she frowned in irritation at the sudden lurch of her heart. What was Kirk doing there?

"He's our house guest," she said with admirable coolness. "Do you want to be introduced?"

Rosemary sagged back in her chair with an exaggerated sigh. "I knew it was too good to be true. Oh, well, at least I know my hormones are alive and well. Go on, take care of him. He's spotted you, and from the look in his eyes, the rest of us haven't a sparrow's chance in a wind tunnel."

Charla's lips quirked. "You do have a unique way with words," she said dryly. She was out of the office before thinking she should have taken time to see if her hair was in place or if her lipstick was still intact.

"Interested in anything you see, Kirk?" she asked when she reached his side.

"That's a charming choice of words," he drawled.

Her lashes lowered as protection from the smoky inspection he was giving her. "We have some attractive turquoise jewelry you might like for someone special back home."

"Digging, Charla?" His voice was silky.

She met his gaze defiantly. "Is there a need to?"

He shook his head slowly. "If there had been, she wouldn't be now."

The tip of her tongue moistened her dry lips. His gaze shifted to hone in on them like a predator who knew what delights lay there. "Is there someone other than Joe Letterman I should know about?"

She gave an impatient shrug. "Joe isn't—"

"I know, honey. But he thinks he is. Is there anyone else?"

Without moving, he suddenly seemed to loom over her. She refused to retreat or turn away from his piercing gaze. "And what if there were? It's no business of yours."

"Honey, don't talk nonsense. You never acted obtuse as a youngster. You couldn't have changed that much. After last night, you know damn well it's my business to know what competition needs eliminating. I don't share my women."

Charla knew her cheeks were flaming. Where had their common sense flown, talking this intimately in the middle of The Trading Post? "This is no place to—"

"I agree. Your father was telling me about this pet hobby of yours, so I came to see what it looked like. And also to ask you to have lunch with me."

Hobby? Charla didn't hear beyond that disparaging word. "I'll have you know that this *hobby* is a viable business concern!"

Kirk watched in fascination as her clear blue eyes shot flaming darts at him. "I didn't mean to denigrate your store," he soothed. "You have every reason to be proud of this outlet you're providing for the natives. We can talk about it more over lunch."

"I'm sorry. This is our busy time—" A cough came from behind Charla, and she broke off to see who was there. Rosemary was sorting through a pile of Chimayó mats, looking suspiciously innocent.

"I couldn't help overhearing the gentleman's offer,

Charla. Of course you can go. I made certain we'd have plenty of coverage this week."

Charla's look was murderous. "Kirk, this interfering female is Rosemary Downs, my assistant. If I didn't need her this week, I'd fire her. Rosemary, this is Kirk Webster, a visiting friend of the family. And I use the word 'friend' in the loosest sense of the term."

Oh, yes, he had charm. He took Rosemary's hand and focused his pewter eyes on her, and that practical woman went into a swoon before Charla's eyes. She should see what his kisses did, she wanted to snarl.

"Charla does have a way with words," he said, smiling at the dazed woman. "Then you won't mind if I steal her away for an hour or so?"

"Heavens, no," was the traitorous reply. "The store has adequate coverage for the rest of the day."

Kirk's smile deepened, and her assistant leaned heavily against the display case. "Rosemary Downs, I owe you one," he murmured to her further bemusement.

Charla found herself tucked into the Jaguar with a vague recollection of her purse being thrust at her and a determined hand placed on her elbow guiding her out of the store.

"Kirk, I will not be manipulated this way!" she stormed as he eased the car into the flow of traffic.

"Hush, honey. You must be hungry. Maria was concerned when you ate so little at breakfast. All I want to do is take care of your appetite."

The glance he gave her caused her heart to perform a disquieting leap. It was evident he'd be happy to do the same for any appetite she wished to mention. What can of worms had she opened by permitting him the intimacy of those kisses?

She forced herself to be honest. Permitted? She'd been an enthusiastic accomplice in that wild rush of passion they'd shared. There was no reason for acting irritable.

"Where are we eating?" She *was* hungry. Her appetite

101

had fled at breakfast when Kirk had sat across from her. There hadn't been enough time to come to terms with the emotions he'd aroused the night before. But that immature reaction was behind her. Good Lord, a woman of twenty-eight should be able to handle a few ardent kisses!

"It's been a long time since I've been to La Fonda. Your father was telling me what an excellent job they did redecorating it and keeping the flavor of old Mexico."

"Some people complain that the Santa Fe restoration committee is going overboard by requiring all buildings in town to be made of adobe. They say the old hotel is enough of a landmark without everything else being done in the same earth color."

"It seemed a little too much of a good thing when I first drove through the other day," he admitted. "I guess, though, that it catches the tourists' attention."

"And the city's main income comes from those tourists," she added dryly. She was fiercely proud of Santa Fe, but she could understand some of the citizens' complaints.

The hostess at La Fonda gave Kirk an appreciative once-over before leading them to a select table. Charla saw him being just as appreciative of the provocative swing of her hips. He grinned unrepentingly when he realized she'd caught him.

"There's nothing wrong with looking, honey. It doesn't mean I want to touch."

"You don't have to explain. I've lived with my father long enough."

His grin widened. "Singly, our fathers must have been hellions in their youth. It blows my mind to imagine what they must have been like together."

"And time hasn't changed them."

Something in her voice sobered him. His hand covered hers on the table, and he waited until she looked up to meet his gaze. "That might be so, but I'm sure that neither of our mothers had any cause to be concerned while they were alive. Do the women your father sees now bother you?"

She looked at him in amused surprise. Did he think she was a spoiled brat, resenting her father's affairs? It wasn't in Charles's nature to be anything but discreet. He was always caring and loving to her. If at times he got her hackles up trying to manipulate her personal life, she knew it was basically because his marriage had been so perfect and he wanted the same for his daughter.

"I'll never forget the terrible year he went through after my mother died. I'm thankful for whatever happiness he can find. I don't know how he'd have made it without your father."

"And you. Don't ever underestimate how much you mean to him."

While talking she'd unconsciously turned her hand and found it held in his warm clasp. There was something gentle yet exciting about the contact.

"Believe me, I don't. I knew he needed me. That was why I didn't set up my own apartment, even with his annoying attempts to marry me off."

His lips quirked with amusement at her exasperated look. "Maybe he was telling you something, that it was time to leave the nest."

"One would think so, but you should hear all the excuses he makes when I suggest it. I really believe he assumes that if I should ever marry, I'll stay. It's all because of that thing he has about grandchildren."

The smile won. "Grandchildren?"

"Don't tell me you haven't been getting the same flack from your father!"

"Tell me about it! Why do you think I set up my business in St. Louis instead of Albuquerque where I'd originally planned? If I took a woman out more than twice, I saw wedding bells in his eyes."

"And, no doubt, hers," she teased.

103

"That's one sure way to make me forget a telephone number," he agreed.

"I see you're still the hunter. You don't know how many older sisters of my friends used to bribe me to find out how to get your attention."

"What did you tell them—that I preferred to do the hunting?"

"Lord, no! I told them that while you pretended otherwise, you really liked being chased. I used to laugh myself silly when you'd tell me the horror stories about how you couldn't get rid of them."

"Brat! I should have realized that you were behind all those pests!"

"I'll never forget that to-do with Ramona Gray. When I told her you were going fishing at daybreak the next morning, I had no idea she'd hide under the blanket in your station wagon. You were so angry I never dared ask what happened when you discovered her."

"It never occurred to her that my father would be going also."

Charla grinned. "I conveniently forgot to tell her that small detail. You'd just gotten your driver's permit, and she assumed she'd have you to herself. What did your father say?"

His lips quirked with suppressed laughter. "There were a few tense minutes. She didn't see my father, and she threw off the blanket when I opened the back to put in the fishing tackle." He paused to clear his throat before continuing. "She must have frozen her tail off while waiting. She had no clothes on."

"She *what?*" Charla couldn't stop the peals of laughter. "Oh, heavens! What did your father say?"

He smiled wryly. "Nothing I care to repeat. I did, however, overhear him later telling the story to Charles. They laughed so hard they all but rolled on the floor."

She dabbed at the tears brought on by her laughter. "I

can imagine. His chest must have been really puffed up. Like father, like son."

He gave her a steady look. "You still haven't changed, have you, brat? I'm discovering a little late just how many of the incidents I had to pay for were instigated by you."

Her grin was unrepenting. "You were always a slow learner."

He glowered at her in warning. "Honey, you're being put on notice. I intend to show you just how slow a learner I am."

The easy rapport changed as if a switch had been pulled. An electrical awareness pulsed between them, making words unnecessary. They stared into each other's eyes, exchanging questions and answers until the waiter came with their order and they had to withdraw their hands.

Charla drew in a steadying breath and speared a shrimp nestled in her seafood salad. What was she being drawn into? Did she want an affair with Kirk? If she did she would have to accept that it would be short-term at best. While the distance between Santa Fe and St. Louis was not prohibitive, it could eventually defeat anything that might be building between them.

She made the mistake of looking at him as he spread horseradish on his roast beef sandwich. The thick crop of white hair was a striking crown for his rugged features. Once when she realized that her friends were swooning over him, she had tried to look at him with a clinical eye. She wasn't quite sure what they saw in him then, but she had no trouble now. The unformed boyish features had matured impressively.

She hadn't known that gray eyes could reveal so many emotions. She'd been scorched by the fire of his anger and had been made boneless when they were cloudy with passion. And like she'd just experienced, they could become endless dark pewter pools that pulled her in, challenging her to sink into them to discover the inner man. Had he ever permitted a woman to touch that vulnerable part of him?

Did she want to be that person? The responsibility of being keeper of that knowledge was awesome. And what did she really know of this man? She had her introduction to Kirk's high libido that proved he was his father's son. His expertise was formidable, and that experience had come from more than books. To get involved in a love affair when they might not see each other for months at a time would never satisfy her, and she could never handle being one of many.

She chewed thoughtfully on a piece of lobster. It all added up to thanks but no thanks. Kirk would have to find his fun and games elsewhere. The food lost its taste, and she drank her iced tea to wash it away.

Kirk wondered what caused Charla's somber expression. He had an impression of time running out, that he better get to know all about her before he finished the problem that had brought him to Santa Fe. There was so much he didn't know about her, and he was suddenly greedy for it all. "You seem to have a good thing going at The Trading Post. Do you make much of a profit?"

"Enough, but that wasn't why I started it. When I finished college and was doing social service work, I saw first-hand that many of the Indians did fairly decent work, mainly in jewelry, weaving, and pottery. But they didn't produce enough to be a dependable source of supply, which is what most outlets require. At The Trading Post we don't pressure them. They bring whatever they find time to make. We managed to end in the black the first year, and it's been growing very nicely ever since. It's evidently something that was needed."

"Very nice, but don't you think you could have turned your money to a better investment?"

Charla admitted to being proud and protective where her store was concerned. Something in his voice made her bristle. "What do you mean?" she asked suspiciously.

106

"You say you did this to help the Indians. It's all well and good, but I bet you don't draw much, if any, salary. If you totaled up the cost of all the running around you do, I bet you'd be in the red." He could feel her resentment and hurried to explain the idea that had just come to him.

"Wouldn't everyone benefit more if your money went to something that better prepared the Indians to enter the work market and make it easier to get a decent job? Too bad you didn't consult someone on this before sinking your money into something that gives such poor return. I know your concern is for the Indians' welfare, but what would help them most is preparation to meet the competition of the hi-tech world. What has made the biggest impact on businesses? Computers, of course. A school teaching them how to use them would have made more sense."

Charla looked at him, stung. "There's more than one way to help them. What I'm doing is helping preserve some of their traditions before they're lost."

"And meanwhile they go jobless, which brings on unnecessary problems."

Charla pushed away from the table. "You'll excuse me, I'm sure. Thank you for the meal, but I better get back to the *useless* store I'm running. No, don't get up. Finish your coffee. With this traffic, it's easier for me to walk back."

Kirk watched in frustration as Charla walked stiffly from the restaurant. Dammit, *now* what had he done? What he had said made perfectly good sense. There was no reason for her to walk out on him.

No woman had ever walked out on him, he groused in irritation as he tossed several bills on the table.

CHAPTER ELEVEN

Charla was relieved to find her father was alone when she joined him for a predinner cocktail. She was still incensed from her lunch with Kirk. First he had the audacity to label her shop a hobby, and then he had denigrated her further by intimating she was low on brain power and should have invested her money in a computer school, of all things!

In a way, she felt betrayed. The boy Kirk, who had been like a brother throughout her childhood, had been more sensitive and would have understood the reasons behind her starting The Trading Post. The man Kirk had become evidently was more involved in the acquisition of the mighty dollar. She went on the premise that there were other things just as important, like people's pride in themselves and their heritage. She was just doing her bit by encouraging the Indians to retain pride in unique skills developed over the centuries. Her store was simply an outlet for the products of their talent.

"Dad, what do you think of this painting I just bought from Mary White Feather?" Charla asked, displaying the square of canvas she had brought with her.

Johnny had framed it in seasoned wood, which brought out the texture of the man's weathered features. The quiet, forever love was even more evident in Mary's husband's eyes. Seeing its glow still created an uncomfortable quiver to the small vulnerable space hidden deep within her.

Charles inspected the painting with interest. "She's always been good with color. I think she's one of the best landscape artists in the area. But I do like what she's doing with her portraits. Do you think she'd be willing to work for commissions? Once our friends see that painting I'm certain some of them would be interested."

"It would depend on her husband."

He nodded with understanding. "Is he off the wagon again?"

Charla sighed. "Yes, and that means she stops everything to devote her time to him."

"Where do you plan to hang it?"

"In my bedroom, for the present."

His eyes lighted with a teasing laugh. "Is that the latest version of 'come up and see my sketches'? It should work."

Charla gave him a despairing look. "Honestly, Dad! I wish you'd get off this grandchild kick I'll get married when and if I ever find a man that can hold my interest."

"Ah, child, is interest all you're looking for?" he asked sadly. "Don't sell love short. It's what brings the sun into life. I found that a man sits with the gods when he can share his love with a woman."

Charla's eyes grew soft with love. "That's just it, Dad. Having seen what you and Mom had, how can you think I could settle for anything less?"

Charles examined his daughter closely. At times like this he was overwhelmed that this gorgeous woman was his daughter. What was wrong with today's men letting someone this lovely remain single at twenty-eight?

He sighed. He knew it wasn't because they didn't try. Hell, ever since she slipped into the teens, the boys had been after her. He'd had many a rough time until he realized she was keeping them effortlessly in line. Her cool lack of interest had held them off, confused. At the time, he'd breathed a sigh of relief, but enough was enough. He'd paraded a bevy of promising men for her selection, hoping one of them would please her. Maybe he'd done wrong in pushing the issue, but a father had to do something to break the stalemate. She was getting too settled in the single life, and that was no way to get those grandchildren!

"I need some legal advice, Dad. Jane Madrinez brought John into the shop yesterday. They still have no idea where his father is. Who should I contact about tracing him down?"

"Why do you want to do that? I don't think finding him will convince him to come up with any support money."

"That's not the point. I'm thinking of the child's welfare. I thought it would be smart to get Big John to sign a release. John's had enough trauma, what with a father deserting him and then his mother dying. Jane is taking care of him now, but once her child is born, she'll be rejoining her husband. I don't know if she plans to take him with her, but he's too lovely and intelligent to be submitted to the uncertainty of the life of a migrant worker."

"From what I've seen of him when you bring him around, I agree. But how do you plan to alter that?"

Charla found herself nervously chewing her lip, then stopped. Her father read body language too easily. "I'd like to adopt him." Apprehension had tightened her throat, and the announcement came out in a whisper. She could tell her father heard by the slight tightening around his eyes.

"I admit I've been pushing for a grandchild, but do you think that's the wise course to take?" he asked with admirable restraint.

"I've been giving it a lot of thought," she said defiantly.

"I'm certain you have. But John is a Hopi. Do you really believe his relatives will permit it? You know how family oriented they are. You must admit that he's well loved. And think of the child. His formative years have been on the reservation. Moving in with us will be quite a cultural shock. Does he need that kind of trauma on top of all the others he's had in his young life?"

Charla bowed her head. Her father was smart, all right. She'd expected him to lay out all the negative aspects of being a single parent and had been prepared. Instead, he'd shown how it would be from the boy's side. She had to admit he'd produced valid arguments. Quietly, with a small sigh of regret, she put her dream aside. It had been tentative at best.

"I guess you think me a fool."

"Never that, my dear," he said gently. "I can understand your reasoning. He's an exceptional child, and I can see why he brings out your love. But there's no reason why we can't keep an eye on him, and when the time comes we can see that there's a scholarship available."

Needing time to adjust to her disappointment, Charla took her drink out to the placito. It was there that Kirk found her when he came down from his room. His approach was wary. After their parting, there was no knowing what fresh barbs she had ready to shoot at him.

She was standing by the small pool, and he was surprised by her pensive expression. The noise from the fountain covered his approach, and she looked up, startled, when he hesitated beside her.

Charla gave him a fleeting nod before her attention returned to the gold fish swimming lazily in the pool. He meant to go on, but something about the droop to her shoulders made him pause. She was hurting, and he fought the desire to gather her protectively close. He was not happy with the thought that his careless words might be causing her distress.

"I stopped here the other day when I arrived," he said musingly. "I'd forgotten all about the pool and how it used to fascinate me as a child."

"We were scolded often enough about splashing water on each other."

"Especially when we were dressed in our good clothes."

Memories had Charla raising her head to smile at him. "Those gold fish always intrigued us. We could never catch

111

them. Remember the time you read me the story about King Midas and how everything he touched turned to gold? We were sitting here by the fountain. When you were finished I insisted that I had that magic touch. Why else were the fish that color?"

She'd been barely six and trying to decipher the words in the new picture book that her parents had bought her. As a treat, she was being taken with them to dinner in town, and she was dressed in a new dress that she adored. To keep her quiet, her mother had handed her the book with strict instructions not to get soiled while she finished her own dressing. Kirk had come along walking stiffly in his Sunday-best clothes. With the supercilious air only a ten-year-old could show to someone younger, he'd taken the book and proceeded to read it to her. She'd been jealous of his accomplishment and seething by the time he finished. Her assertion about her magic powers was in retaliation.

Kirk was bemused by the laughter in her eyes. Then memory of the event returned with startling clarity. The other day he'd only recalled the part of falling in the fountain. "You pushed me in, didn't you? I was determined to show you you were wrong and leaned over to catch one of the slippery things. The next thing I knew I was falling head first into the fountain."

She laughed. "I had to. You were acting like you were God's gift to the world. I decided you needed a little cooling down."

"I recall feeling decidedly uncomfortable after my father ran out to see what the screaming was about and saw my dripping clothes."

"I got caught in the splash, too," she admitted. "It seems we hardly got out of the doghouse when we were back in for something else. We had to stay behind, and I remember hating you with an unending passion. Remember the Lakes? I'd heard that they were going to be at the restaurant with their son, Tony, who I had a powerful crush on. I had planned to seduce him with my new clothes."

Kirk's laughter was barely withheld. "If I remember that dress, it had layers and layers of skirts and petticoats. How did you plan to accomplish a seduction wearing all that?"

She waved a hand dismissively. "At six I wasn't concerned with such minor details."

His laughter came then, a roar of appreciation that Charla couldn't help joining. Charles watched with vast satisfaction from the living room. Just wait until he told Tyson! What better than shared laughter to tear down barriers?

They were caught, allured by the lights in each other's eyes and the laughter ringing in the air. His long finger brushed a vagrant strand of hair from her cheek. It was a light caress, but the electricity in it sent shivers coursing through her. The corners of his firm mouth indented in an acknowledgment of the effect he had produced.

She swayed slightly and her eyes darkened, bringing a groan to Kirk's throat. "Keep looking at me like that, honey, and I won't care if your father has a front-row center seat watching us." Her eyes closed in a fleeting look of distress. "I know," he commiserated. "Tell me, are you always chaperoned this well?"

Her smile was strained. "It appears that way, doesn't it?"

"It's beginning to look like a challenge."

Her smile widened as she recalled their conversation over lunch. "And you always thrived on the hunt. Are you putting me on notice?"

Long lashes hid his gray eyes. "What do you think?"

"I won't let it be easy."

"It will make the capture all the more enjoyable."

"If there is one."

"Have no doubt, princess. The traps are already being laid."

"I'm good at evading them. I've had several years of practice with some very good hunters."

"But not by one who has years of experience learning what made you tick."

"I was a child then," she scoffed. "I'm a woman now. I've learned ways of evasion that you've never heard of."

"We agree on one point, at least. You're very much of a woman."

Charla drew in a sharp breath. Her body immediately tingled with memories of how his mouth and hands had discovered how much of a woman she was.

"Trap number one," he murmured with satisfaction when he saw the flush tinting her cheeks. "If I took you in my arms, how long do you think you'd be able to resist?"

Charla flared at his arrogance. Unfortunately for the retort burning her lips, Maria announced that dinner was ready. She stalked away, fuming over being unable to do a little much-needed slashing at his inflated ego. So he thought her a pushover, did he? She glared, aware of the devilish laughter glinting in his eyes. Oh, yes, he was his father's son. She should remember that and be on her guard.

Her tension slowly faded during dinner as her father regaled them with humorous events that had happened during the golf tournament. She knew she was overreacting to Kirk's teasing. It was just one more piece of evidence pointing to how he could send her emotions into erratic highs.

By the time dessert was served, the general laughter had her forgetting her resolve. So when Charles mentioned that the combo she adored was back and there was a dance being given at the club, she accepted Kirk's invitation to attend. She loved dancing and wondered if his fluid stride was an indication that he was as good a dancer.

She decided that the blue silk jumpsuit she wore was adequate. After slipping some essentials into a small purse, she joined the men in the living room. She wondered at

Kirk's mocking expression until he suggested they leave. When her father accompanied them to the door, she thought nothing odd. Her mouth dropped open when he slid into the backseat of the Jaguar.

"There's more room back here than I thought," Charles marveled breezily. "I'm glad you decided to go to the club. I'm in the mood for a card game."

"Having trouble with your car?" she asked sweetly. His innocent look wasn't fooling her. What was the old reprobate up to now? She'd have thought he'd be rubbing his hands in glee over getting them off together.

"It was making a few odd noises," he confessed. "Guess I'll have to have it checked out."

She believed that like she believed elephants flew. If his Lincoln gave a burp it would have been in the garage within the hour.

"How did he work that out?" she asked Kirk later when he led her to the dance floor.

Kirk grimaced with wry amusement. "Very simply. He invited himself along. It's a little awkward telling one's host to go jump in the lake."

"Tsk. Feeling outmaneuvered by the chaperon?" she asked slyly.

His hands rested on her hips while absorbing the beat of the music. "It's early yet. Your father is making it difficult not to accept the challenge."

Her hands slid around his neck. "Am I being put on the alert?"

"It might be wise, unless you're ready to concede defeat."

Her eyes laughed up at him. "Darling, the war has just begun. That trumpet you hear is really the bugle calling the reserves to arms."

"Speaking of arms, I like the way yours feel around me."

They were moving to the sensuous rhythm of the bossa nova. He was a better than good dancer, she quickly discovered. His hands were warm on her back, holding her so their bodies made frequent contact.

It took only two turns around the dance floor to make Charla conscious of the increased tripping of her heartbeat. The touching was like stoking a furnace. She was suffused in a warmth that matched the heat radiating from his body. Rather than repelling, it attracted. When the music slowed to a languid rhythm, the pull became too strong. She folded against him with a sigh of resignation. Who was she fooling? In spite of their teasing, this was where she wanted to be.

His arms closed around her. She was tall, the top of her head reaching his eyes. It made the blending of their bodies a perfect match. How could limbs that felt so weighted still move to the music? she wondered as she collapsed closer in a need for total contact.

"I don't think this is such a good idea." His groan was a whisper in her ear. "As it is, I'm going to have a hard time walking off this floor."

She was all too aware of his physical response. Her breasts were aching, and she knew he was aware of her own highly charged reaction.

"Perhaps if we dance to our table?" The lights were low and should give them some cover.

"I'm taking you to the door," he warned. "We're getting out of here."

She had no objections. The room was suddenly stifling. She wanted the cool night breeze on her face. They made it to the outer foyer only to discover Charles was there talking to a departing couple.

"Have enough dancing?" he asked cheerfully. "That's good. I didn't find a game going, so I'm ready to go home when you are."

If she wasn't feeling identical frustration, Charla would have laughed at the way Kirk's jaw bulged when he ground his teeth.

* * *

The frustration still haunted her later when she prepared for bed. When they reached the house, Charles outdid himself playing the host. She finally conceded defeat and went to her room, conscious of pewter eyes burning into her back.

The need for Kirk's kiss was a physical ache. Was this what he meant about falling into trap number one? If so, it had been sprung, all right, and for now, she hadn't the energy—or desire—to escape.

CHAPTER TWELVE

Maria was placing a serving of eggs Benedict in front of Kirk when Charla entered the dining room. She stared at the plate with distaste. Her restless night had taken away her appetite.

"I'll have juice and a bowl of cereal," she informed the housekeeper. When she left, Charla filled her cup from the insulated carafe. "I see that Maria is still into the prodigal son bit and is enjoying pampering you."

Kirk examined her, gauging her feelings. Had her night also been long and frustrating? "All pampering is received with open arms."

His double meaning wasn't lost. In spite of her intentions to ignore him, she found her gaze drifting across the table. It was definitely the wrong thing to do. In the clear morning light, his eyes were more silver than pewter. They trapped her, held her mesmerized. Warm shafts of heat raced through her body, causing her breasts to feel heavy, her body to pulse with painful awareness.

Maria brought in the juice and cereal. Her presence, thankfully, broke the hold he exerted. Charla stared, dazed, at her breakfast. How had he done that? Without touching, she'd been touched. Her body reveled in the glory of his caresses. If he could do that with just a look, what would it be like to be in his arms without the hindrance of clothes to separate them?

It took several deep breaths before she could trust her

hand not to tremble when she reached for the glass of juice. She was already lost if she accepted his premise that they were indeed destined to become lovers.

"Charla."

She shivered as her name wrapped around her in a husky whisper, revealing that he, too, had felt the incredible reaction. It took all her courage to move her eyes from his hands clenched by his plate. She didn't know if she could survive another inundation of those electrical sensations.

Her gaze slithered up over his broad chest. Immediately, her breasts became further engorged as memory returned of their painful state when pressed against him dancing the previous night. Her stare shifted quickly, only to be arrested by the curve of his treacherously sensuous lips. They were slightly parted as if poised, ready to accept her kiss.

Kiss? It was already an aching need. The desire to have his mouth possess hers was an ache that forced a small whimper to her throat.

The sound surprised her, and her gaze flew to his to see if he'd heard it. He had. His eyes glistened with silver highlights, illuminating the passion, the intense desire. She gloried in the knowledge that it matched her own.

"Ah! Glad to see you two haven't left yet. I was afraid I'd missed you. I got interested in a book last night and didn't put it down until well after one."

Charla stared uncomprehendingly at her father as she struggled with the abrupt end to the intense emotional touching she just shared with Kirk. She was acutely conscious of the thundering pulses racing through her, the erratic panting her breath made as it slipped through her parted lips.

"Those eggs look good," Charles commented, hoping his smug satisfaction wasn't showing as he took his seat. "Maria does them well. Do they meet with your approval?"

Kirk had to clear his throat twice before managing an

answer. "Everything Maria cooks is excellent. You don't know how lucky you are to have her."

"But I do, I do," he returned enthusiastically as he reached for the coffee carafe. "Thank goodness I've finally been able to convince her to have someone in to do the heavier housecleaning. She's never told us, but as far as I can figure she's pushing seventy. I prefer to have her energy expended in the kitchen."

Kirk ate mechanically. He knew from past experience that the eggs were done perfectly, but he was still struggling with the bewitchment Charla had performed. Her head was bent as she scooped the cereal from the bowl. He suspected she was having no better luck at tasting her food.

He longed to have her look at him, to again be singed by the passion flaming in her eyes. But that would be fatal with her father sitting there expecting him to join in an intelligent conversation.

A ray of sunlight beamed through the window to place its benediction on her. It created creamy shadows under her high cheekbones and along her slender neck. His gaze dropped lower, and his breath caught as the ache hit his loins.

She was wearing a snug top with her jeans, and the bright light delineated the sweet curves of her breasts. Centered on each mound was a raised peak, accented by the shadow it cast. His mouth was dry with the need to close over them, to finally taste all the flavors of this woman. If he didn't get out of the room soon, he was going to make a fool of himself, Charles or not.

Maria brought in the eggs, and Charles attacked them with gusto. Charla pushed away her half-empty bowl and rose, giving her excuses. Kirk hurriedly drained his cup and dropped his napkin on the table with forced casualness and rose also.

"I better be on my way, too." Sensing that Charles wanted to prolong the conversation, he added quickly, "I want to give the warehouse another going over before I give you my initial report."

He reached the door in time to take Charla's arm and steer her into the living room and away from prying eyes.

"Your father is involved with his eggs, and I daresay Maria will be kept busy in the kitchen for a few minutes." He smiled at her look of surprise. Did she really think he could let her go without doing what they both wanted, needed?

His arms went around her, anchoring her loosely in their circle. "Good morning, princess. I think it's time to greet you as you should be, the way I wanted to the moment you came into the room."

Her hands pressed against his chest in a momentary hesitation before they decided on their own to glide over his shoulders and clasp behind his neck. It was time to be honest with her desires. "Yes, I think you're right."

Her smile held no guile. His breath caught at its beauty. The conviction came that here was a woman worth loving, but it was fleeting. His primary need was to once again feel the softness of her lips under his, to probe beyond and taste the nectar waiting there for him.

Knowing his hunger was as strong as hers, Charla was surprised when his kiss held none of the demand she'd half expected. His mouth moved seductively over her lips, telling her that he wanted her to enjoy the exchange as much as he.

He spent tortuous minutes nibbling and sucking before soothing the soft curves with the tip of his tongue. It wasn't enough. Charla was beside herself with the need for more. His control was a new frustration. How could he tease like this and hold off giving her full satisfaction!

Her hands dug into his thick hair in an effort to stop his wandering teasing mouth. Feeling his resistance, she pulled her head back in surprise to look up at him. The fiery passion blazing in his eyes momentarily stunned her. But then, wasn't she experiencing the same intensity?

121

"Tell me what you want, Charla."

All of him. Her throat ached to say the words. The desire was easy to read, and Kirk closed his eyes briefly, savoring the joyous satisfaction the knowledge brought him.

"I know, love," he soothed. "So far our timing has been pretty lousy. We'll have to do something about that."

Yes, Charla admitted freely. But for now . . . "Kiss me, Kirk. Really kiss me," she said.

A low groan hummed in his throat as his arms tightened in response. How was it that she could so easily send him skyrocketing out of control? Her lips were parted and his tongue plunged between the barrier in answer to her demand. The waiting feast was unbearably intoxicating. He explored the richness, drank heavily of the taste, and drowned happily in the essence of the woman. And as he took, he gave, reveling in the knowledge she was doing her own enjoying, hovering on the brink of the same ecstatic sensations.

There was no existence but the one they were creating. Wrapped in its cocoon, the peal of the front door bell went unnoticed as did the sound of Maria hurrying to answer it. The voices slowly filtered in to alert them that others did indeed exist besides themselves.

Kirk reacted first. His head raised slowly, and he shook it in need to clear his senses of the obliterating fog. "What the devil?"

Charla blinked at the change in his expression. She turned her head to follow his gaze. Her body tensed in surprise.

Tyson stood by the fountain, gesticulating while talking to Charles. At his feet was a matched set of suitcases. What in the world was Kirk's father doing there, complete with luggage?

"Of course you're welcome to stay!" Charles's voice boomed across the courtyard. "I should have asked you

122

before. Most of the day Kirk is busy at the plant, but at least this way you can see more of him."

"My sentiments exactly," Tyson answered.

"If you don't want to share the bathroom with Kirk, take the room further down the hall," Charles said as he took one of the cases and dropped it by the stairs leading to the upper bedrooms. "Leave your bags here for now. I daresay you've had breakfast, but join me for a second cup of coffee. Too bad you didn't come earlier. You missed the kids by about fifteen minutes."

Charla breathed a sigh of relief as the two men entered the dining room through the sliding court doors. Thank heavens they hadn't been seen, lost in that devouring kiss and wrapped around each other as if they were one!

"Did you know your father was coming?"

"Not the slightest. It would be interesting to know what brought him to that decision."

She wondered at the frown bringing his dark brows together. "As Dad said, we should have thought about inviting him. You haven't had much time to visit with him."

"I'd planned to do that when I had more of a handle on what's going on at your father's plant. I'd just as soon he hadn't come." Seeing her surprise, he exploded. "We're having enough trouble with two chaperons. We certainly don't need three!"

Charla felt as if she had been hit in the chest. Of course! How could she have been so dense? How could she have thought that their parents had dropped their original plan? The building anger was welcomed. It was easier to handle than the frustration left behind from the aborted kiss.

"I was right in the beginning!" she seethed. "Don't you see what they're doing? Those two are up to their ears with their usual plotting. Haven't they learned to leave me alone? I don't need any of their devious schemes!"

Kirk was momentarily stunned. Eyes that short minutes ago were burning with passion were now flashing with fury —and aimed at him. Did she really think he was involved

123

in their maneuverings? Before he could mount a rebuttle, she was out of his arms.

"Just stay away from me, Kirk Webster," she warned as she headed for the door. "Practice your seduction on someone more gullible. I'm certain your father won't care who you marry as long as you produce the required grandchild."

She stormed out of the house, leaving Kirk muttering a stream of oaths that blued the immediate area.

He glared after her. For a moment, he considered confronting Charles and Tyson, then decided that with his anger barely under control it was wiser to follow her course and leave. It was bound to explode if he confronted the conniving renegades. He'd tell them off that evening after he had cooled down.

Catching a glimpse of red as he tore down the driveway, he realized Charla had taken her Porsche instead of the van. When they hit the highway, he sped after her and was forced to admire her handling of the car. His Jaguar had far more horsepower, and it would have been easy to pass her, but he throttled the idea. In her present mood she'd take it as a challenge and he didn't want any accidents.

Kirk didn't blame her for her anger if she had to endure the type of interference from her father that he got from Tyson. He'd definitely become gun-shy from those "accidental" meetings arranged by his father.

But wasn't she one gorgeous creature when she was blazing with self-righteous fury! Her eyes were breathtaking when shooting flames. And her skin! Emotion brought a lovely flush to her golden skin.

Her cheeks had the same blush when he kissed her. For an unguarded instant, he envisioned her body bathed in that rosy glow when blending with his. An oath exploded when his body tightened in response. The sorceress was doing this too often to him. It was time he worked on springing trap number two.

He resisted touching his horn in a farewell as he took

the turnoff to Treemont, Inc. He didn't know if she'd realized he was following her. The knowledge might spur her volatile anger and make her drive even faster as she continued into town.

If she expended that kind of energy in his arms she'd be a dream come true, Kirk thought as he parked the car and headed into the plant.

Rosemary eyed her employer warily as she stormed into the store. She'd rarely seen Charla in a temper, and this one looked like a hair raiser. Perhaps it would be prudent to disappear with some excuse until it blew over.

"You, er, had a bad night?" she asked hesitantly.

Charla glared at her. Bad night? Her nights as well as days were out of synch ever since that white-haired cretin had come roaring up her driveway.

"Nothing that a few aspirin won't cure," she muttered, pressing a slender finger to her throbbing temple. These emotional highs and lows he put her through were taking their toll. The fact that he could produce such an effect sent her anger a spin higher.

"The bottle is in the top drawer of the desk," Rosemary told her sympathetically. "I made a fresh pot of coffee. Why don't you relax in the office with a cup and give the pills a chance to work? I can handle the customers. Things are a little slow right now." Her educated guess was that that dynamite of a man must be behind Charla's mood. He was the type capable of sending a woman into ecstasy or despair.

Charla emerged from the office an hour later. It had taken that long to come to terms with what had triggered her stormy reaction. If her thinking ability hadn't been so decimated, she would have realized that Kirk was as leery as she over his father's sudden appearance. Hadn't he intimated he was just as resentful of his parent's attempts at manipulating him up the church aisle?

Somewhere during the hour, she was forced to be honest

and admit she wasn't as much against letting what was developing between them run its course as she pretended. There was no denying that Kirk was downright sexy, with a charisma proving difficult to turn away from.

Her reevaluation at least accomplished one thing. It alerted her to what the old codgers were up to. She liked her life-style, her freedom. She had nothing against marriage, but it would take a very special man to make her consider entering that state. And at this point she couldn't see her old childhood chum being the one.

True, his sense of humor matched hers. It had been years since she had shared real laughter with anyone.

And talk. Their conversations ranged over an endless number of subjects. They even had fun switching viewpoints midstream just for the stimulation of a fresh approach.

As for appearances, he was outrageously handsome in a strong, masculine way. Not that it mattered. His personality was what one remembered.

And his kisses . . . They sent her to outer space. Lord, did they ever do that!

She stopped abruptly, disconcerted by the list she was itemizing. If she weren't careful, she'd be selling herself on the man. Determined to banish the path she was following, she hurried into the shop. There was work to do, customers that needed taking care of. That's what was important in her life.

She'd told Sally not to come to work and was therefore surprised to see her standing hesitantly by the front door. Her stoic expression didn't hide the worry in her eyes. Charla hurried to her. Was Pete causing more trouble? He had no history of drinking, which was why his lapse at the warehouse had been such a surprise. She'd always liked the couple. They were so proud of the house they had built, of the baby due that month.

"Is something wrong, Sally?" Charla asked.

The woman's gaze dropped to the floor. "I need to talk to you," she whispered. "Alone."

Charla frowned. Something was definitely bothering the woman. "The office is impossibly crowded. We got a new shipment of kachina dolls, and we haven't finished pricing them. Why don't we go across the street for some iced tea?"

Sally glanced quickly over the room. "But you're busy. Perhaps it's best that I come back another time. It no doubt isn't important, anyway."

Charla looked at her consideringly. It must have been very uncomfortable coming into town in her condition. Whatever was bothering her, it must be important. "The extra help is here to take care of them. Wait until I tell Rosemary where I'll be."

Five minutes later they sat in a booth in the coffee shop sipping the iced tea. It was evident from Sally's worried expression that she was having second thoughts about what had brought her there.

"Is it something about Pete?" Charla asked gently. Was her worry over whether he'd be fired? "Was he unable to go to work today?" It seemed likely. Considering the low level in the bottle, he must be nursing a mammoth hangover.

Sally's head shook in denial. "He's back, and he asked me to thank you for what you did for him. We both do. He also said to tell you that he doesn't know how the bottle got there, that he never took a taste from it." Her round face firmed with pride. "He would never drink, especially when he was working. The job you got for him means too much to us and our son. He would never do anything to risk losing it."

Charla smiled in sympathy. Of course Sally believed her husband's excuses. It was vital to their marriage. But that didn't explain the bottle found with him. "That's all right. At least he managed not to lose a day at work. Just tell him not to get into any situations like that again. I doubt I'll be around to help him."

Sally tried to lean forward to give more emphasis to her words. Her face darkened with frustration when her swollen belly prevented her from bending closer over the table. "You're not understanding. Pete never drank. He was fine an hour after you left. He thinks he was drugged!"

Shock made Charla blink. "Drugged? Didn't Pete realize that taking drugs could be far worse than going on an occasional bender?"

The woman slid awkwardly from the booth, her face expressionless. "I told Pete you wouldn't believe me," she muttered. In spite of her burgeoning body, stiff pride accompanied every step as she left the shop.

Charla watched her leave, sympathy her primary emotion. It must be difficult hanging on to one's pride when faced with a husband whose excesses might cause the collapse of one's dreams. While at times she longed for a full love, she certainly didn't want it if it was at the cost of her own integrity.

But what was she to do with Sally's story? She didn't see how it altered what Pete had done. If she remembered to, she guessed it might help to discuss it with Kirk. He must have some information on how other companies handled drug problems.

When he entered the plant no effort was made to alert Harvey Stone that he was there, and Kirk wondered if it was Charles who had Letterman pull off the guard dog. He moved swiftly to the warehouse section, not unaware of the curious looks that followed his progress.

Kirk was surprised to find Pete Fallen on the job. He evidently had exceptional recuperative powers. Considering the condition he had been in the day before, Kirk would have sworn it would have taken several days for him to dry out.

The day before, a thread of an idea had hit him. Then

128

Charla had appeared, and as was becoming all too apparent lately when she was near, his thoughts took off on tangents that had nothing to do with the business at hand. Now he hoped to recapture the thread and see where it led him.

"I see you're feeling better," Kirk said conversationally.

The Indian looked at him warily. The man looked vaguely familiar. Had he been the one to help Miss Treemont get him into her van? She'd given his wife a quick rundown on how he'd been spirited from the plant so his job wasn't jeopardized. He was in her debt for getting him this job, doubly so after she rescued him from the strange thing that had happened to him the previous day.

"Is there anything I can help you with?" Should he be talking to this man? He looked around for Larry Perkins, his foreman, but didn't see him. In fact, he hadn't seen him since sharing coffee during their break.

"If you can spare a few minutes, I'd like you to show me your procedure from the time the invoice arrives until the order is ready for shipment."

"That's easy. I'm doing one now, so you can follow me." He waved toward a small office near the delivery door. "I pick up the order there where Perkins pegs them on the wall. If it's large, I take my cart and fill the order from the shelves." He pointed to the lot number and name of the articles in each slot on the heavy-gauge shelves. "They come from the plant in their fitted boxes, so I just have to pack them securely in the shipping crate. The label is already printed and comes with the order sheet, so all I have to do is see that it gets pasted on securely."

Kirk frowned. It was a simple procedure. With the parts already individually packed and sealed, how did someone manage to replace one that passed inspection with one that was defective? It could only happen if Pete was in on the scheme. Or—and that was what had hit him the day before —if Pete were slipped a bottle to get him out of the way whenever the switch was made.

Charla had been adamant that he did not drink. If that were true, it wouldn't take much to have him pass out. A feathering excitement shivered through his stomach, an alert signal he'd learned to listen to that he was on to something. The problem was how to get Pete to confess to the dates of the times he'd crawled into a corner until he could function again. If they coincided with the time frame of those bad shipments, Kirk would be halfway home.

CHAPTER THIRTEEN

In spite of additional aspirin, remnants of the day-long headache still lingered. As a result Charla opted to let her hair hang free. Even the weight of a braid hanging down her back produced too much pressure. She smoothed the black silk toreador pants over her long legs before tying the bright red bow on the loose-sleeved white silk blouse. Matching red lipstick was brushed on her lips, and she stepped back from the mirror to check the results.

It would have to do, she decided, and left her room to cross the placito to the living room where the men were enjoying predinner cocktails. She was tired and had put off the confrontation long enough. Her day had been long and hard, and she just wasn't up to the sparring that awaited her.

If the town weren't jumping with tourists, she'd manufacture an excuse to go off on a vacation. As it was, The Trading Post was exceptionally busy, and she was hard put contacting her suppliers to maintain an adequate inventory.

Kirk was replenishing the older men's drinks when she halted silently at the entrance. As if he had a special radar tuned to her, his head snapped up and he stared at her. His pewter eyes lingered in fascination over the dusky fall of hair cascading down her back. Then they blazed a special message of greeting. It took all her willpower not to respond in kind and return it with a cool warning. Didn't the fool realize they were being watched like hawks?

"Ah, there you are, my dear," her father greeted her. "I was about to send Maria to see if you'd fallen asleep."

"A few more minutes and I might have," she admitted, bending over to kiss him. She then turned to greet Tyson with a brush of lips over his cheek. "It's good to see you again. It's a shame that the problem at the plant is taking so much of Kirk's time. At least being here you'll have more of a chance to talk with him."

Charles beamed. "My sentiments exactly. I thought it only right that he stay with us."

That wasn't how it had looked that morning, Charla thought sourly. Her father had been as surprised as they were to see him arrive with bag and baggage.

"Martini, Charla?"

She turned to find Kirk inches from her. From some reserve, she dredged the strength not to eliminate the intolerable distance that separated them, to permit her body full contact with his.

"Not tonight," she managed. "I'm fighting a headache, and I think a club soda would be better."

"It's that store of yours," Charles accused in annoyance. "You're letting it take up too much of your time. You're never at the club anymore. I know you don't care for golf, but you were tournament quality at tennis."

"Bob Seymour and Ted Jackson have been asking about you," Tyson added. "Not to mention a long list of others. They miss you at the courts."

Charla waved a dismissing hand. "I know. They keep calling. They can't seem to understand that unlike them, tennis isn't my whole life."

"But there's the other side," Charles remonstrated. "The Trading Post shouldn't become yours."

"Ignore them," Kirk said, offering her a glass filled with club soda and ice. "They've forgotten how it was when they were busy building their little empires."

She accepted the glass and found her hand enclosed in his. In some magical way its heat managed to extend and wrap warmly around her, cradling her in his protection.

How did he do that? she wondered, shivering slightly when he withdrew his hand. She took a hurried sip from the glass, using the time to regroup her shattered attention. What in the world had they been talking about?

By the time dinner was over, Charla wondered if she'd overreacted again. All her senses were on high alert, but she could find no innuendos in the conversation, no exchange of overt or sly looks. To all appearances Charles and Tyson were enjoying the evening together and were content to have their children with them.

"Headache better?" Kirk asked in a low voice as he sat beside her on the sofa. Their elders were in heated discussion over the advisability of placing additional sand traps on one of the fairways to make it more interesting.

"Much," Charla admitted. "An early bedtime should take care of what's left."

"An early bedtime would take care of a lot of both our problems."

His heated gaze made her swallow. "Oh? How interesting. You must be one of those who believe that problems can be resolved in sleep."

The corners of his eyes creased from his smile. He found he thoroughly enjoyed these small duels. "Correction. I'm a firm believer that, asleep or awake, a large variety of problems can be solved in bed. I'll be happy to demonstrate it to you."

"I have no doubt you would," she returned dryly. "Why do I have this feeling that it's the awake part that you're primarily interested in demonstrating?"

"You always were quick on the uptake."

Did he have any idea how sexy his smile was? "I found early on that it was necessary to develop that ability in order to keep ahead of you. You always acted so damn

133

arrogant and superior when we were growing up. My greatest pleasure was taking you down a peg."

His eyes widened with mock concern. "Me, arrogant? Superior? It must have been my defense system working overtime. It seems there was this brat who was always hell bent to get into situations. Like the time you stole into the henhouse and tried to crawl into one of the nests."

Her eyes lighted with mirth. "You remember that? I always wondered how you caught on to what I was doing."

"Good Lord, how could I not? The poor chicken was cackling in outrage over being ousted from her nest. Hearing the noise, I thought I'd better investigate. You were a mess. You had egg yolks all over your legs."

"And you took the blame," she said softly. She'd forgotten that. At the time, she was furious at him for spoiling her experiment.

"I never did ask. What in the world were you trying to do—hatch the eggs?"

She nodded sheepishly. "I loved the soft downy chicks. I thought if I hatched a batch of my own, my parents would let me keep them to play with."

He threw his head back and laughed. The full-bodied sound stopped the older men's argument in midsentence. Two heads turned to see what they were missing. Happy to find that their children were enjoying themselves, Charles and Tyson were unable to hide their satisfied smiles.

Kirk saw Charla frown. Sensitive to every change in her, he looked at the men and made the same evaluation. The old reprobates! It seemed Charla had been right in her assumption, after all. His anger wasn't directed at them for what they were attempting, rather on how Charla would put up barriers now that her suspicion was reactivated. Damn it all, he'd worked hard to get past them all. If they fouled things up now, they'd answer to him!

Wanting to castigate them with snarling accusations, he instead cadged a cigarette from his father and went out to

134

the courtyard to smoke. By removing himself, he hoped to get a handle on his resentment.

He sat on the bench by the fountain. The smoke curled lazily over his head as he stared somberly into the cascading water. Imprinted was the picture of Charla as he had left her—her lovely lips set with rebellion, her face a frozen mask. It was all wrong. Her incredible blue eyes should be laughing as they had been minutes before. Better yet, they should be heavy with passion, her lips red and dewy from his kisses.

Think, brain, he ordered. He was proud of his ability to turn events to his benefit. The gift had come to his aid innumerable times, saving him from making a wrong and costly move. He needed that intuitive power now. It hadn't been a line when he'd informed Charla that they would be lovers. She had become a necessity, a reason for breathing.

The shock of that realization held him spellbound for long minutes. Dear God, had it finally happened? Was he really in love? The gradual acceptance of the idea had him chuckling at the puckish twist fate had dealt him. Who would have believed that his childhood nemesis—that lovable, obnoxious brat—would be the one to finally floor him? After all their parents' plotting, it seemed they had finally hit the jackpot. The celebration should rate the best bottle of champagne from Charles's superlative wine cellar.

He ground out the cigarette and was half off the bench before reason had him sagging back on it. So he admitted he was in love. Great! But it took two to tango. What about Charla? If the expression on her face were a barometer of what she was feeling, he was in deep trouble.

Come on brain, he thought. It was imperative that he come up with something before her barriers were so entrenched that he'd need a lifetime to break them down. He didn't have that lifetime or even a week to waste. His patience wasn't the best when he desired something as much as he wanted her, needed her.

Charla managed to keep her seething resentment under control. She dearly loved the two old codgers, but why couldn't they mind their own business? What was happening between Kirk and her was still too tender and susceptible to bruising. Even in this embryonic stage, it was creating wonderful havoc with her nerves. What a shame if it died unborn because of the irritation caused by their fathers' constant interference.

Her headache was back, and she used it as an excuse to leave for bed. The lights illuminating the inner court hadn't been turned on, and she was startled when she saw a dark shadow move by the fountain.

"Come and join me." Kirk's quiet order was an invitation floating on the still-warm night air.

Charla hesitated. She was truly tired, but some nuance in his voice urged her to comply. "For a few minutes," she tempered.

She'd forgotten how narrow the iron benches were. She was sitting much too close and was immediately aware of the heat of his body, the lingering aroma of the cigarette he had smoked.

The moon hadn't risen as yet, she noticed, but the thousands of stars twinkling in the black velvet sky gave off enough light so she could see his profile. His square jaw made him look aggressive, but his expression was somber, and she wondered what he was thinking.

Kirk took her hand and traced the outline of each finger with an intensity of feeling. They were long and slender, with each nail filed modestly short as her work demanded. There was strength there, too, he knew, a strength that was an integral part of this wonderful intriguing person.

"You're right. Our parents are up to their usual crazy plotting."

"Oh?" Charla replied, struggling to concentrate. His caressing exploration of her hand had obliterated the lingering irritation.

"As you said, at first it was amusing, but it's been going on too long and has become irritating."

"I couldn't agree more." Was he thinking, as she, that what was happening between them needed the freedom to develop without interference?

"So what are we going to do about it?"

" 'Do'?" She turned her head to look at him with surprise. "You tell me. I've done everything but move out. Is that what you're suggesting?"

"You really don't think that will work, do you? The usual parade of hopeful offerings will continue whenever you return to one of his parties."

Charla sighed in agreement. "So what do you suggest we do?"

Kirk paused. This had to be done carefully. Charla was no fool. The audacious idea had sprung full born in his mind when she'd stepped out on the flagstone.

"We agree that we're tired of our fathers urging us to do our trip down the church aisle, right?"

"Right!" It was an enthusiastic agreement.

"We love and respect them but would dearly like to teach them a lesson, right?"

"Right." The enthusiasm was slightly tempered. What was he leading up to?

Mentally, he crossed his fingers. "Now comes the nitty-gritty part, and believe me, I've given it great thought. Why don't we pretend to go along with their plotting?"

"What do you mean?" The enthusiasm was put on hold.

"I mean that we put on the act of our lives. We pretend to fall in love, let them believe that their conniving has finally paid off. Knowing them, they'll be boasting to their friends. Then, when there's no way they can back out, we'll act out a big breakup scene and go our own ways. We'll think of a way to do it so they'll realize that in the future they better keep their noses out of our lives. The only way for them to learn is to be tripped by their manipulations so they fall flat on their faces."

"I—I don't know if I can do that."

His arm slid behind her on the back of the bench. "Honey, I found that you can do anything if you want it badly enough. Good Lord, do you want to spend the rest of your life evading the latest of their choices? Remember, princess, I saw your reaction several times. This headache that's been with you today, can you honestly say it didn't originate when you saw my father arrive this morning with the obvious intention to help your father manipulate us? Why should you be put on the rack like that? I prefer to do my own searching, and I'm sure you do, too."

She had to agree with him on that point. "But I hate the thought of hurting either of them."

"Believe me, I do, too. But they're made of strong stuff. The whole object is to discourage them from interfering with our personal lives."

"But you'll be here for such a short time. I don't see how we can hope it will work."

She hadn't backed off with a flat no. He wasn't home free as yet, but his breathing wasn't as constricted. Sweet Charla had no idea how much he intended to accomplish in that time. "My vacation is for two weeks. We should have things well under way, and if necessary, for something this important I can extend it."

"I don't know . . ."

He turned to face her. It was time to use other, more potent persuasion. "Honey, I hate to see how miserable you feel over what they're doing. Let's give it a chance, hmm?"

He was so near that her lips were seared by his breath. She needed space to come to terms with what he was suggesting. Something wasn't quite right, but the tingling was already starting, obliterating coherent thought. The need for his lips on hers was all she could concentrate on.

"Kirk?" It was a tiny gasp, asking, begging.

"Yes, honey. Oh, *yes!*"

His lips found hers and he tasted of excitement, of hunger. Of Kirk.

Then there was just the exquisite delight of knowing he was enjoying their kiss as much as she. Her hands ran feverishly over his shoulders to luxuriate in his thick mane of hair. His kisses covered her face, her throat, her ears. He loosened the red tie, and his fingers made short work of opening the buttons of her blouse. His hand smoothed the exposed skin, delineating the limitations set by her lacey bra. She was bathed in the increased heat from his body, and suddenly she needed more.

She tugged the knit shirt free of his pants, thoroughly enjoying how the muscles of his back grew taut under her hands. Her fingers splayed, the better to feel, to memorize all of him. They circled his broad rib cage before moving up over his chest where she ran her fingers through the light curls. She found his male nipples and teased them, and his body twitched from the resulting spasm.

"Princess, the things you do to me!" He pushed her bra up, too impatient to find the closure. His mouth was a hot moist demand over the tight bud. It brought a whimper to her throat that she buried in his bent neck.

The protruding decorations on the unyielding iron bench pressed painfully against her spine. It was sharp enough to bring Charla back from the throes of delight. She never knew from what hidden well she dragged up the words to deny the desire to drown again in the exquisite passion he was creating.

"Kirk, please, you have to stop!" she cried. "We can't go on like this out here!"

She felt the shudder go through him. He paused and rested his damp forehead on her chest. Her fingers ran gently through his hair, the caress telling him she understood his need to regroup. Drawing in a deep breath, he raised his head to place a tender kiss on her swollen lips.

"It's always the wrong time, the wrong place." Even in the subdued starlight, his eyes were bright with the passion

139

he was fighting to bring under control. "It's time to change that and take charge."

Trembling with her own fight for control, Charla had no answer. She adjusted her bra, and he pulled his shirt down to tuck it back in his trousers. Seeing her fingers were having difficulty with the buttons he'd undone, he pushed her hands away. A kiss was placed on each section of exposed flesh before hidden by the next closure. When he was finished she fought the crazy urge to rip them apart so he could start over again.

"I don't think I can walk," she whispered.

His teeth gleamed in the starlight. "I know. I'm having much the same problem, and I have to climb a flight of stairs."

"Poor baby," she commiserated playfully. She stroked his arm and felt the muscle twitch in response. It wasn't fair to tease him this way.

"Never mind 'poor baby'! If you had any feelings, you'd think of an alternative for me."

Which meant her room. She pulled in a quick breath, imagining him there, lying naked beside her on her queen-size bed.

Charla rose quickly to her feet. "I have complete faith in your ability to manage those stairs."

"Chicken!" he teased in a husky whisper.

His soft throaty laugh followed her to her room.

CHAPTER FOURTEEN

Charla started her solitary breakfast, wondering why she was up so early. She'd awakened at dawn with Kirk's crazy proposition to outwit Charles and Tyson filling her thoughts. Now, away from his charismatic presence, it was easy to poke holes in his preposterous idea. Had she really consented? She couldn't remember. A shimmering haze covered the rest of the time by the fountain, brought on by his devastating kisses.

She had showered and dressed, and by the time she reached the dining room her determination was firmly in place. She had two strong reasons for not going through with his idiotic plot. First of all, she had no acting ability. It wouldn't take her astute father long to see through the stupid act. But the second reason was more important. She was fully aware of the pull Kirk had on her. She'd already discovered the dazzling effect brought on by his kisses. She'd end up by tumbling into his bed without a whimper.

Whimper? She'd be racing him to it, tearing off her clothes in her eagerness!

Kirk entered, tall, broad-chested, and so obviously in control of his life. It was evident that he hadn't been spending hours with his mind squirreling on an endless treadmill.

"Hello, princess," he greeted her, and before she could do a thing, his arm snaked around her waist to lift her from her chair, and his mouth closed over hers in a long, thorough kiss.

"Now I can think about breakfast," he said with satisfaction when he released her. He bent to pick up her chair that had fallen over and sat her on it with courtly deference. "Do you always look so beautiful this early in the morning?" he asked, filled with a masculine approval over the swollen pout to her lips.

"Do you always greet your hostess like that in the morning?" she countered.

He looked properly horrified. "Decidedly not. That's reserved for my true love, the one I intend to marry."

Charla's hand pressed over her breast to still her crazy heartbeat until she realized this was all part of his playacting. "That's what I want to talk to you about."

His strong hand raised in protest. "Uh-uh. We made an agreement last night, and I'm not letting you back out of it. A promise is a promise. You'd never think to renege when you were a youngster."

Had she promised? "But I don't think I can carry the act out," she protested.

"Don't worry, honey. I'll do all I can to make it easy. Just follow my lead."

She looked at him suspiciously. His smile was too much like the ones their fathers produced when they were up to something. Which, in a way, Kirk was.

"As we agreed last night, time is of the essence, so we have to get on with our plot. I have to check on something at the plant this morning, but I'll pick you up around eleven and we'll go on a picnic."

"Picnic?" she yelped. "Are you out of your mind? I have too much to do at the post."

"Did I hear picnic?" Charles asked, coming into the room. "I say, what an excellent idea. Haven't been on one in years."

Kirk gave him a sour look. "Charla and I are going on a

142

picnic. I haven't explored the hills in years, and we decided to do some tramping around."

Charles reached for the coffeepot. "Oh, in that case, I'll forego it. We get enough walking done on the golf course. Don't we, Tyson?" he added as his friend joined them.

"What, walking? We certainly do," he agreed genially. "Do you think Maria will object to making me one of her delicious Spanish omelets?"

"I'll be happy to," Maria said, coming through the swinging door from the kitchen with glasses of fresh-squeezed orange juice. "All three of you?"

The other men quickly agreed to the treat. She paused to fill the coffee cups before taking the carafe to bring fresh. "By the way, Kirk, the picnic basket is packed."

Charla arched an eyebrow as Kirk gave his thanks. So he had it all planned, did he? It was time to puncture his balloon. The stormy words formed but were forcibly swallowed when she caught the eager expressions on the men watching them. Didn't they ever stop? she railed to herself.

It was just that attitude that had brought Kirk to suggest his crazy idea. She stifled the rising anger and tried to deal rationally with the problem. Nothing was going to change unless they did something so outrageous that these two men were shocked into being forced to drop the whole subject. Considering the number of so-called eligible men her father had paraded in the past, she could envision the line continuing into eternity. Kirk was right. She was tired of the constant irritation it caused. It was reaching the point where she was flaring up at the slightest provocation. Maybe his devious plot had some merit. At least it had the potential of succeeding where her vocal objections had failed.

"Uh, I think I can be ready by eleven for that picnic," she managed. "Which means I better get going to clean up as much work as possible."

She dropped her napkin and left, wondering what she

was letting herself in for. She was too irritated to notice the various degrees of satisfaction on three male faces.

"So that handsome hunk is taking you away from it all," Rosemary teased when Charla informed her she would be leaving early.

"No one is taking anyone away from anything," she returned coolly. "He used to hike all over these hills and wants to revive a few memories."

"Careful over what else he wants to revive. Anyone looking like him doesn't have to take those hikes by himself!"

"Don't tell me that you're intimately acquainted with those hills yourself?" Wasn't it said that attack was the best defense? "I've seen those handsome men that live at your pueblo."

Charla was amused at the deepened tint to Rosemary's dusky cheeks and the sudden change of topic. It looked like those barren hills were witness to more than the obvious.

By the time eleven came, Charla was annoyed at herself for frequently checking her watch. She tried to tell herself the anticipation was because she hadn't been on a picnic in years.

Who was she trying to fool? she finally thought. Rosemary had hit it right on. Kirk certainly could be labeled a handsome hunk. But, oh, he was so much more.

Remembering the emotions he aroused so effortlessly by his kisses had her fumbling blindly through the account sheets. They'd be spending the afternoon off in the hills without the chaperons he grumbled about to snap them back to earth. Was this to be the time, the place he'd stated more than once was due them? Heat washed over her, and she drew in a shuddering breath. He had primed her well. She knew she wouldn't have—didn't even want—any defense if that was his plan.

And then Kirk was there, wearing well-worn jeans and a

lightweight football jersey. The sleeves were pushed up, exposing his strong forearms and their covering of black hair. No one should look that sexy, Charla thought. She grabbed her pocketbook and, calling her good-byes, hurried him out of the shop before Rosemary could come up with one of her embarrassing remarks.

He grinned as he helped her into the Jeep. "That's what I like, a woman who can't wait to be with me. And, yes, this belongs to the company," he informed her when she eyed the vehicle questioningly. "Your father okayed it. Said it made more sense than taking my Jag, considering the state of some of the roads."

"That would hurt him more than if one of us sprained an ankle or something else as careless," she admitted, knowing how careful he was about his own car.

They headed north on a highway and turned off on a secondary road before reaching Pojoaque. Straight ahead was the mountain range crowned by Baldy Peak soaring up more than twelve and a half thousand feet.

"I hope that's not what you plan to climb," Charla protested. "I'm not in shape to do that kind of strenuous hiking."

He spared her a glance from the rutted trail they were now navigating. His teeth flashed in a decidedly lecherous smile. "Don't worry, honey. The condition of your shape has been taken into consideration."

She decided she wasn't about to touch that remark and focused on the scenery. Although she'd never come this way before, it was the usual landscape that she loved. No cloud moved in the vault of the clear blue sky. The hot summer sun held dominance over the arid red earth. The silver green sagebrushes provided scattered oases of visual relief. The only shade was that made by the buttes. It was past noon and she was hungry, and she wondered where he hoped to find a shady spot to eat.

As if on cue, her stomach grumbled and she looked at him expectantly. "I assume you heard that. I'm being notified that this is supposed to be a picnic and you promised food."

He frowned as he checked the position of several buttes. "Soon, my love, if they haven't moved the damn thing."

"Then you *do* have a special place you're heading for." The ground was strewn with stones of all sizes. She had assumed he was simply searching for a spot that wasn't too rocky.

He looked slightly indignant. "Of course. Would I abscond with you without a definite place in mind? I think this is the turnoff. Hold on!" he ordered as he spun the wheel and headed to one of the buttes.

Charla managed to catch hold of a grab bar before being jarred out of her seat. As far as she could see, there wasn't a hint that another vehicle had ever traveled this route. She glared at him. This place better be better than special!

He rounded the steep side of a flat-topped hill and braked. The cloud of dust billowed over them. When it settled, Charla's face was filled with wonder.

Extending from the side of the butte was an exquisite stone arch. Framed in its graceful curve were the mountains that lay ahead, with Baldy Peak holding dominance over them.

"How lovely!" she breathed.

"Special enough for you?" he asked, feeling inordinately pleased to find she was as overwhelmed by the beautiful phenomenon as he'd been when he'd first stumbled on it.

"Oh, yes. I've seen arches before, of course, but they were usually eroded by water. I don't see even a dry gulch here."

He stepped out of the Jeep and handed her the blanket while he took the picnic basket Maria had packed. "Come on," he said, extending his hand. "I'll show you what else is special about it."

She was surprised to see the width of the arch. Three cars could easily drive side by side on it. As a result it cast a wide shadow under it in which she was happy to stand.

The short walk in the sun had brought beads of moisture to her forehead.

"Feel anything?" he asked as he tossed aside several stones to make a smooth area for the blanket.

"There's a breeze! It forms a breezeway!"

He nodded with satisfaction. "I've been here only a few times, but even if the air was still elsewhere, there was always a current going through here."

Charla sat on the blanket and rested her chin on her drawn-up knees. She looked dreamily over the land, letting the quiet and peace settle in her. What problems had Kirk been wrestling with that he had felt the need to come here in search of an answer?

"You feel it, too, don't you?" He joined her with a hand braced on the ground behind her.

She nodded in agreement before turning her head to thank him for sharing it with her. His face was inches from hers. Blue eyes met gray, and his hand slid up to curve around her nape. His lips hovered over hers in hesitation, as if knowing that after this, nothing would be the same again.

Their breaths mingled, already one. Then with a groan rumbling deep in his chest, the space was eliminated. He took her mouth in a grinding possession that told of passions held in check too long. Charla understood the reason and reveled in the small pain. She was suffering from the same frustration and hunger.

Kirk was appalled at the intensity of the kiss. He hadn't intended to come on like an animal, but like an animal, his first overwhelming need was to put his brand on his female to show her she was his alone. He eased the pressure, then dampened her lips to soothe them before sipping gently of their soft fullness. He could feast on them forever, tasting the fine nuances of her nectar, enjoying the textural differ ence of her tongue, the smooth lining of her mouth.

And her skin! Pure satin. Was there ever anything so sublime? His fingers caressed her cheek, the exposed line of

147

her throat. The neck of her shirt was an obstruction they refused to recognize. The buttons were quickly undone, and the delight of finding she wore no bra sent a spasm straight to his loins.

The shirt was pushed off her arms, and he pressed her back on the blanket. It was the first time he could see her, and he examined the firm fullness of her breasts with pleasure. The deep rose nipples were already tightening, and he dampened a finger before rubbing them lovingly. "My hands told me how beautiful you were, but I had to see in full light," he said huskily.

"And what about me?" she asked just as huskily, tugging at the jersey tucked into his jeans.

He sat up to unsnap the jeans and pull down the zipper in order to release the material. It was pulled off over his head in one impatient tug. Her hand slid over the taut skin at his waist before traveling up his chest and brushing over the hair covering his breasts. Her finger flicked over a nipple, and he felt the jolt of pleasure shoot through him down to his center.

"You're very sensitive, aren't you?" she murmured, delighted to discover she wasn't the only one.

"As you are," he admitted. He lowered himself over her, bracing his weight on his elbows. "And before this afternoon is over, I'm going to know every sensitive spot you have on your body." His grin was a promise of untold delights that awaited them.

Passion was already darkening her blue eyes. "And I fully intend to show you a few that you haven't discovered yet."

Could she, she wondered? He'd had plenty of opportunities to discover all his erogenous zones. She tossed the thought away. There was something special about how they sparked off each other, and that attraction would make all the difference.

He watched her eyes darken further as he rubbed his

chest lightly over her breasts. "We'll have to see, won't we?" he whispered in challenge.

She bit her lip at the sensations he was producing even as her body arched in supplication for closer contact. When her moan whispered between them, perspiration broke out on his forehead from the strain already exerted on his control. He'd wanted this first time to be perfect, but she was already pushing him to the limit. It was then a race to remove the rest of the restricting clothes. Free at last, they fell back on the blanket to lock each other in a fierce embrace as they kissed with wild abandonment.

"Charla, love, please," he gasped while raining kisses over her face. "I've been in torture wanting you in my arms. I can't control myself much longer."

In answer she wrapped her legs around him, telling him in the most elemental language what she thought about control.

He entered her with a slow smooth thrust and caught his breath with the pure joy of at last being enclosed in her silken warmth. She was his, he exulted with a possessiveness that had him opening his eyes in surprise. Her eyes were wide, and in their smoky depths he saw the same joy and wonder. For a startling moment, he felt his throat tighten and tears burn his eyes.

The distraction passed when her hips moved to accommodate him better. The slow rhythm began that, when it reached the heart-thundering culmination, brought them to an exquisite explosive release.

Their cries of joyful triumph soared to the sky.

CHAPTER FIFTEEN

Charles's chuckle was loud as he worked the handle on the golf ball cleaner. "You should have seen your son's face when I said I thought going on a picnic was a great idea."

Tyson's grin was wide. "I wish I'd been there. I bet that shook him up more than a little."

His friend removed the ball from the soapy solution and dried it before giving it a critical inspection. "Shook him a little? His look was confining me to the nether regions!"

"I wonder what Maria packed? Remember the great picnics she used to prepare for us?" Tyson's voice was filled with nostalgia. "We used to have great outings. I'm glad to hear that they aren't considered too old-fashioned by the new generation."

They teed off, and it wasn't until they putted out the hole that the conversation was resumed.

"I wonder where Kirk took her?" Tyson contemplated as they waited for the foursome ahead of them to finish teeing off.

"I was wondering the same thing. We had that river at the ranch with plenty of trees to give shade. But I don't know where they'd go around here."

"Kirk must have had *some* place in mind. Or do you really think they plan to hike like they said?"

Charles gave him a telling look. "Did you raise your son to be an idiot?"

Tyson glanced at his watch and grinned. "No, and if

he's anything like his father was, the mission should be accomplished about now."

The skin grew tight around Charles's eyes, and he drew in a long slow breath. This was his daughter they were talking about, but when she had gone to college he had had a long strong talk with himself. There'd be no hovering. After Greta's death, he'd brought her up with love and the best values he could. He guarded his independence and had offered the same freedom to her. His one prayer was that life would be generous with her.

Because his marriage had been so perfect, he sincerely wanted the same for her. Perhaps he'd been wrong in bringing the string of potential husbands to her attention, but they had been carefully vetted. Had he done wrong bringing these two together? While he loved Kirk as a son, he'd seen little of him for the past ten years. What if he considered Charla fair game and returned to St. Louis without a backward glance after he solved the mess at Treemont, Inc.? Once he and Tyson thought of their off-spring as a perfect match, it never occurred to them that they wouldn't fall in love.

But that was silly. Anyone could feel the electricity that sparked between the two when they were together. He'd seen how Charla's eyes were constantly drawn to Kirk. But what if it were one-sided? Charles squirmed, for the first time wondering if his manipulations might bring the pain to his daughter that he'd prayed wouldn't happen.

The balls were fished out of the last cup, and the golf cart was taken to the pro shop. "I still get a charge over how you piled in the car with them the other night when they came here to dance," Tyson mused with a chuckle as they went into the clubhouse. "Kirk must have wanted to strangle you."

Charles's face beamed with devilish glee over his success. "I don't know how chaperons used to take it. It's most uncomfortable knowing someone wishes you were in Siberia."

"I think things are going well enough that we can dispense with that chaperoning idea," Tyson decided wisely. "Too bad you didn't have the patio lights on last night. I swear they were doing more than talking by the fountain."

"Whatever happened, it had Kirk hotfooting to Maria before going to bed about fixing that picnic basket. From Charla's show of surprise this morning, he hadn't told her about it."

Tyson grinned. "That's my son, using the old head."

They looked up with smiles when a couple stopped by their table. "Hello, Nancy, George," Charles said in greeting. "Didn't see you at last week's tournament. Been away?"

"Congratulate us," Nancy beamed. "We just got back from Los Alamos. Our daughter gave us a perfectly gorgeous granddaughter!"

"I thought my kids were something else, but this one's a honey," George eulogized, pulling out his wallet. "I took some Polaroids of Delilah. Wait until you see her."

Charles and Tyson spent ten tortuous minutes agreeing with the proud grandparents' assessment. They looked sourly at each other when their friends decided they'd milked their attention dry and went off to fresh fields.

"Just wait until our first grandchild comes," Charles muttered into his glass of beer. "I'll sky write it and ram the announcement down all those sickening grandparents' throats."

"I intend to send singing telegrams," Tyson countered, not to be outdone. They grinned at each other, realizing their silliness. "By the way, I heard a great band at an anniversary party I went to the other night. They played a nice mixture of dancing music. I got their card. If you get a chance to hear them, do it and see what you think."

Charles swallowed a bite of his thick corned beef sandwich. "I put an order in for the champagne for the wedding. Do you think ten cases will be enough? We better start on the list of people we plan to invite to make certain we don't have duplications."

The white notebooks came out as they made notations. "Did you hear the name they tagged on that poor baby?" Tyson finally asked in disgust.

"Yeah, Delilah. Can you imagine when she gets to school what the kids will do with it? Why couldn't they give her a nice clean name like 'Kim.' " Charles's eyes lighted up. "Kim Webster. Hey, that sounds good! I think I'll add it to the list." He flipped to the back of the pad and penned it under 'David' and 'Greta.'

"We'll have to come up with another boy's name to balance it out," Tyson stated, copying the list in back of his pad.

"I bought this great book on names. It gives the origin and meanings and all their offshoots," Charles said, taking a bite of the pickle that accompanied his sandwich and savoring the clean sharp taste. "Remind me to show it to you when we get home."

"You know, we haven't thought of possible places for them to go for their honeymoon."

"I took Greta to Hawaii."

"They've both been there several times."

"True, but this time it should be different."

They exchanged matching grins.

"I should hope so. Of course, there's Acapulco—or that great place we once went to at Lake Tahoe."

Tyson ran his finger down the list he had compiled. There was still a lot to be done. He had every intention that this wedding would top the social events for the year.

Hell, the decade, if he had his way.

CHAPTER SIXTEEN

Kirk put the picnic basket in the back of the Jeep, then took the blanket from Charla and tossed it in. She went to open the door and climb into the Jeep, only to find herself anchored to its side with his hands braced on the door and his body pressing against hers.

"Not so fast, honey," he murmured huskily. "I need one last kiss for the road."

She had no objection. How could she when every inch of her was so finely attuned to him? They'd dozed lightly after that first wild and glorious mating of their bodies, then had come together again with a slow, tantalizing sweetness. Their other hunger then had demanded fulfillment, and they had dug into the picnic basket to enjoy the food Maria had packed.

The woman had outdone herself. They ate heartily of the cold spiced chicken that was another of Maria's specialties. The marinated slices of ruby red tomatoes disappeared quickly. Dessert was a bowl of fresh fruit. All was washed down with a tangy dry white wine. It had been a feast to please the gods. And they felt kin to them, sitting in the shade of the arch with the desert breeze caressing their unclothed bodies.

After repacking the basket, it was the most natural thing in the world to lie down on the blanket with her head on his shoulder. Then, as if in need to see if it had really, after all, been so spectacular, hands touched and marveled over

154

how quickly they had memorized all the special erotic zones, and senses quickly soared.

When they came together it was like in a perfect duet, the refrain a blend of harmonizing beauty. With every part of them singing, they reveled in the beauty of the melody they were creating and soared with the music to its grand climax. Afterward, they lay in each other's arms, listening with a sweet regret over its passing as it was carried away on the sighing breeze until even the echoes had faded.

Charla was amazed that now, pressed against the car door, Kirk's kisses were still able to bring the heated yearning to such a high pitch. With his body pressed to hers, she felt his own response.

He groaned, resting his forehead on hers. "What you do to me is pure witchery."

"You're not so bad in that category, either," she whispered with a breathless laugh.

"You make me feel like a randy kid."

"No, randy man," she corrected with an exaggerated leer.

He grinned down at her. "Whatever." He eased slowly away from her. "From the set of the sun, the afternoon is pretty well shot. We better leave, or I won't be able to see the trail out of here."

Her hands remained around his neck. "Would that be so bad?" she suggested seductively.

He gave her a swift hug before pulling from her arms. "Oh, honey, don't even suggest it. I can't think of anything I'd like more. But can't you see our parents sending out the troops, thinking we met with an accident?"

She could, all too clearly. Giving the stone arch one last lingering look, she climbed into the Jeep. "Thank you for sharing it with me," she said, gazing at the spectacular natural structure as he inserted the key in the ignition.

He paused, squinting at the mountain framed by the arch. It was a thing of beauty. The lowered sun highlighted

155

it with gold and gave the deep purple shadows added emphasis.

"My pleasure, princess. Now I know I was saving it to share with someone special." He brushed a kiss across her soft lips delightfully swollen from his lovemaking. Giving a sigh, he started the car. Any more of that and he'd take his chances and take her up on her suggestion. One thin blanket might not offer much protection from the cool desert night air, but with the heat they were so adept at generating, that might be of no concern.

She smiled at him, hugging the sweetness of the thought to her. Conversation became impossible as they bounced over the stony soil. The jostling was little better when he picked up the faint trail. In comparison, the road when they reached it made it seem they were riding on a cloud. His hand reached for hers and he nestled it on the hard surface of his thigh. The touching made talk unnecessary. Communication was at some subliminal level, and it held them enthralled.

Charla couldn't recall ever regretting reaching home, but this time the sight of the hacienda was synonymous with the ending of what had been so perfect between them. It was with a feeling of dismay and apprehension that she withdrew her hand. By that simple act, the real world reasserted its presence.

"You might as well go home early," Rosemary said tartly. "You've been staring at that column of numbers for half an hour and haven't totaled it yet. That must have been some picnic lunch Maria packed for you!"

Charla looked guiltily at the ledger before her. After wandering aimlessly around the shop throughout the morning, Rosemary had sat her at the desk and told her she might accomplish more there. It hadn't worked. She kept seeing that incredible arch curving over her, felt the wool blanket under her, and more mind bending than all, kept reliving kisses that had seared right to her soul.

They had managed to steal a kiss that morning in the garage before they went their separate ways. The chaperons had been up before them and were ensconced in the dining room, so they could do little more than send silent messages at breakfast.

When, in desperation, Kirk had suggested to Charla that they go to a movie that night, Charles had perked up and said it was a capital idea. He'd see what was playing and they could all go after an early dinner. He seemed immune to the loaded look Kirk sent him. Tyson had saved the moment by reminding Charles that they were expected at a club meeting on the fate of the golf course. It was odd how though she suspected her father was teasing, the resentment she usually felt failed to materialize.

"I must have gotten too much sun," Charla prevaricated, closing the ledger and sliding it back into the drawer.

"Could be," Rosemary agreed, not hiding the amusement in her eyes. "You didn't fall, though, did you? Your face looks more like it's been rubbed with sandpaper."

Charla's fingers touched her face before she looked at her assistant with disgust. Kirk had a moderately heavy beard. She had shivered with delight when he had drawn his chin over the tender flesh of her belly. That morning when applying lotion, the slight sting alerted her that the tiny bristles had left their mark on her face as well.

"I can do without your sense of humor," she told her friend. "Don't you think you better see that the customers are being taken care of?"

"Will do, boss lady. But I mean it—everything is under control here. There's no reason why you have to hang around."

"In that case, I'll go," she said, surprising the woman. "For the past month, I've been running around like a mad woman to make certain we have enough on hand this week for the tourists. My father says I deserve some free time, and I think he may be right."

That was what she wanted, Charla admitted when starting her car. The free time gave her the opportunity to drive to Treemont, Inc. This time she planned to see what changes had been made. And just maybe she'd see a tall, prematurely white-haired man with broad shoulders and lure him to lunch.

The guard recognized her and gave her a broad smile while waving her through. She had just parked the car when she heard the low growl of a motor and saw a long black car race by. Her spirits fell when she recognized Kirk's Jaguar. It was just her luck that he'd taken off early.

The Jag slowed at the gate, waiting for the guard to check its occupants through. It gave her time to see the black frown Kirk was wearing. She was further surprised to see Pete Fallen by his side, his expression apprehensive.

In an instant her euphoria collapsed, and Charla came crashing back to reality. What was Pete doing in Kirk's car, and why were their expressions strained? Had Pete blown it again? Had Kirk found him hidden once more behind the boxes? This time there was no surreptitious slipping the man from the plant as she had done in order to save his job.

Anger shook her, anger that Pete was so self-centered to risk his wife's happiness, especially with the baby's arrival so close. But the main shaft of her anger was aimed at Kirk. The look on his face boded ill for the man sitting fearfully by his side. She had explained the home situation. Was Kirk riding a high horse, thinking of reporting Pete and making an example of him? His apparent uncaring attitude was so diametrically opposed to the image of him in her heart that finding he had feet of clay made her feel nauseous.

By the time she turned her Porsche around and passed by the puzzled guard, there was no sign of the black sports car. That left her with no idea of which direction Kirk had taken.

Now what? She'd just seen a Kirk that she could not relate to. The day before, she had seen a warm and caring man. She had given of herself completely and had believed all sorts of crazy things were possible. Had she been foolishly blinded by thinking what they shared was something special to him? To have her dreams collapse so totally left her feeling devastated.

Bitterness left an acidic taste in her mouth. How naive she'd been in falling for his talk about pretending they were in love to confuse their parents. She realized now that she'd acquiesced so easily because a part of her was already fantasizing over the idea. She sorely wanted to go home and crawl into bed. There, with the sheet over her head, she could retreat from the world and the death of her dreams.

Instead she turned the wheel and headed away from Santa Fe. She'd make the rounds of her feeders in the various pueblos and see if they had anything ready for her shop. Keeping busy was the answer. It should help lessen the bleak emptiness seeping into her heart.

Earlier, Kirk had left Charla, savoring the kiss they'd exchanged in the garage. He had risked indulging himself, knowing how it would leave him with a raw need for more.

The day before, he had learned what was meant when it was said that until sex was experienced with love, it was impossible to know its full emotional range. What he and Charla had shared under that sweeping arch had been incredibly beautiful. It was like finally being given a perfect diamond; once seeing its clear, sparkling brilliance, no man-made replica could ever duplicate it or satisfy.

With an effort, he tore his thoughts from Charla and concentrated on the problem before him. He had to find a way to get around Pete's guard. He was certain that the Indian had information, perhaps without knowing it. He also needed to talk with Larry Perkins. The warehouse foreman was very hard to locate.

He was in luck. He found Perkins in the small office near the outside loading bay. He was a thin and wiry man, around five feet eight with sandy hair and pale hazel eyes that regarded him warily.

Kirk could understand that reserve. Something as serious as the loss of the government contract would have an adverse effect on them all.

"Kirk Webster," he said, extending his hand to the man with the introduction. "Is that fresh coffee I smell?" he asked with an appreciative sniff. On a small table in one corner a coffee machine was emitting a mouth-watering aroma.

"Larry Perkins," the foreman answered, giving the hand a perfunctory shake. "Yeah, I'm a coffee buff. Can't stand the stuff they pass off as coffee in the cafeteria. This is a French blend I'm trying. It'll be done shortly if you'd like to try some."

"I'd appreciate it. I bought a chicory blend when I was in New Orleans that I haven't had a chance to try." It was the opening he needed to get the man to relax. They talked about the relative value of chicory for several minutes until the brewing coffee was done.

Perkins took two ceramic mugs from the shelf and fished a styrofoam cup from its plastic package. "Sorry, but I only have two mugs," he apologized.

He filled the cups and called "Come and get it!" to Pete, who was pasting labels on packages.

Kirk inhaled the full-bodied aroma with appreciation before tasting the coffee. Pete joined them and gave him a brief nod before taking a cautious sip from his mug.

"I was here yesterday. You weren't around, so Pete was kind enough to show me the general procedure you go through at this end."

Perkins's wariness returned. "Yeah, well, I guess I was up at the office checking on one of the invoices."

"You seem to have a nice simple and straightforward operation here."

"I find that's the best. Less chance for a foul-up."

"I see you have several boxes sitting under the table. Are they a special order?"

Perkins glanced at them. "Naw, they've been banged up, see?" He pulled one out to show the caved-in corner and the puncture in the side. "When we get a call from the different sections that they got a stack ready to come out here, Pete takes his forklift and gets them. They don't always set them up right, so one or two of the packages gets dented. Mr. Treemont used to be a stickler about not sending any out in that condition. Mr. Letterman hasn't said anything different, so I continue the policy."

"What do you do with them—throw them out?"

Perkins looked at him in horror. "Of course not! They get returned to the proper section to be reboxed. We only carry the large crating containers here for final shipment."

Kirk glanced at Pete as he emptied his cup. He rinsed it out and replaced it on the shelf before picking up the next order form and leaving. He hadn't spoken one word.

His gut warning system was telling him that he was missing something, but he couldn't guess what. He placed the information on hold to review the exchange carefully when he had time.

The phone rang and he stepped out of the small cubicle to give Perkins privacy to answer it. The nagging persisted. What was he missing?

The phone was slammed down and Perkins stuck his head through the door. "Hey, Pete, that was for you. Do you know a store called Panchew? It came from there. It seems a neighbor's boy just came running in saying your wife's gone into labor. She refuses to go to the hospital. Said you'd wanted to know."

Pete's face paled. "That crazy woman! What's she doing going into labor? She's not due for another week. She knows I want her in the hospital. But, no! She insists she wants our son to be born at home, the Indian way!"

He looked blindly at the sheet of paper crumbled in his

161

hand. He tossed it on the table before staring at his boss, his face taut with determination. "I have to get home, Perkins. I have to be with her."

"Sure, I understand. But how are you going to get there? You hitch a ride with some other fellows from your pueblo, don't you? If you take the truck, how will they get home?"

"I'll take him." Once Kirk got over the surprise of his offer, he realized it was natural enough. He could relate to the man's anxiety. If Charla were expecting their child, all hell wouldn't keep him from her side. The unexpected comparison stunned him. Their child. The possibility thrilled and scared him. He didn't have time to consider further. Pete was already reaching for a battered Stetson and was starting out the loading bay.

Not until he waited impatiently for the guard to pass him through did Kirk remember that he'd hoped to get to The Trading Post and spirit Charla to lunch. The hungry need to see her again hadn't abated; in fact, the separation had intensified the feeling, and he frowned darkly over the lost opportunity.

Pete gave him directions, and Kirk floored the gas pedal. It usually took Pete an hour to get home. But that was in an old truck. Kirk's Jaguar was made to eat up the miles and he would get him there in half the time.

They turned onto a dirt lane, and Kirk winced when his car bottomed as it hit a rut. Pete was beside himself with worry. He was practically leaning into the windshield as if by doing so he could assist with the speed. After climbing a rise, a small boxlike house came into view. A ramshackled van sat in the yard with two small children playing in its shade.

A mule was tied in the shade cast by the house. It raised its head as the Jaguar approached followed by a trail of dust.

"Thank God. Matia is here," Pete muttered.

He was out of the car before Kirk could set the brake. An ancient crone blocked his entrance at the door. Her seamed face cracked in a toothless grin. "So you have come, Pete Fallen. Well, you did your part well nine months ago. The time has come to see the results, eh?"

"I want to see Sally. Is she all right?" he shouted in frustration.

"Fathers!" she mocked. "They can be more of a problem than the mother. Don't worry. My daughter is with your wife. When the time comes I will assist her. It won't be much longer." A thin scream came from behind her and she reentered the house.

"That was Sally," Pete whispered in agony. His face was shiny with perspiration as he raked his hand through his hair.

"The daughter, is she equipped to do this sort of thing?" Kirk asked. His mind boggled over how they would manage to force their way past that guardian if they had to abscond with his wife to get her to the hospital.

"She's had training as a midwife," Pete explained, straining to hear anything further.

Kirk felt perspiration break out on his own face. He'd never been this closely connected to an actual birthing. He had admired his friends' newborn infants with a bachelor's restraint when, armed with a gift, he'd paid his respects. But this was different. It was elementary and ageless, with the sun beating down on them and the hard-packed earth under their restless feet. Matia's grandchildren played quietly as if they'd witnessed the bringing of new life into the world countless times.

His tension grew along with Pete's as he paced restlessly in endless circles. Then, after what seemed like hours, but which proved later to have been only fifteen minutes, a thin wail came from the house. Color drained from the new father's face and he stopped in midstride. Then, with a giant leap he ran to the door. He stopped there, his body straining to obey the unspoken command. No one was allowed to enter until the ancient gave the nod.

The wail became stronger, and after the longest ten minutes Kirk hoped he'd ever have to endure, Matia came to the door. In her arms was a small bundle wrapped in the ancient papoose way. She raised it as if in an offering.

"You have a fine son, Pete Fallen. Come, you may hold him for a few minutes before I put him to his mother's breast. See how hungry he is!"

Kirk saw a little round head and a lock of thick black hair. He had a glimpse of chubby red cheeks and a tiny rosebud mouth opened in a hungry quest. Pete was trembling violently as he went up the steps. The woman placed the infant in Pete's arms and made a sign over them both as if in a blessing. He stared long and hard at the miracle he had helped create. But the baby was hungry, and he let out a lusty howl.

"He's an impatient one," the old crone said with satisfaction. "When he learns to control it, he will go far." Smiling indulgently, she took the baby to his anxious mother.

Pete came bounding down the stairs, beaming. "Did you see him? My son! Did you see him?" Tears were running unabashedly down his cheeks as he grabbed Kirk's hand to pump it.

Only then were they aware of the car pulling to a stop beside the Jaguar. Kirk never thought to question Charla's being there. Pete's enthusiasm had spilled out over him. Unaware of her gaping at their jubilation, he opened her car door and practically pulled her out.

"What do you think about that?" he cried. With a large grin, he swept her into his arms. "We've got a boy!"

And then the fantasy returned, slamming him with the image of Charla pregnant, of having a son, their son, and he pulled her close as his mouth took hers with a passion she was powerless to resist.

CHAPTER SEVENTEEN

"What in the world are you doing with a book on baby names?" Charla asked in amazement, picking up the paperback and flipping through the pages. They'd finished breakfast and she'd gone to the living room to retrieve the shoes she'd left there the night before.

"Remember the Henrys?" her father replied. "They just came back from visiting their new granddaughter. They named her Delilah, and I remembered having this book. It lists the meanings of names, and I wanted to check. What do you think of labeling a child like that?"

"I think that's putting a load on the poor kid," Charla said, imagining the teasing she was bound to suffer through.

"That's what we thought," Tyson agreed. "If you ever have any children, what would you like to call them?"

Kirk Tyson Webster, Jr. The name almost slipped from her tongue. After experiencing the jubilation accompanying the arrival of the Fallen baby the previous afternoon, and especially after the exuberant kiss Kirk had given her, she couldn't help fantasizing over how that usually controlled man would react when his own son were born. She could see the baby. Would he have black hair? And maybe her blue eyes? The picture had danced through her head all evening.

"Oh, I don't know. I like Mom's name, and I always thought 'Sylvia' pretty, or 'Eric.' I don't think I could take another 'Charles,'" she admitted, "or 'Charla.' That would be too much of a good thing." Her eyes narrowed. Why this interest in names for babies? The men had shifted to another subject, and she was disgusted with the return of her paranoia. She'd succumbed too often to it in the past. She was ashamed of her negative reaction when she had seen Kirk drive away with Pete. She only hoped he'd never find out how quickly she'd been ready to accuse him of all sorts of things.

Driving to the store, she realized how sorely she regretted that there had been no opportunity for a private exchange that morning. It was shocking how quickly Kirk had become important to her well-being! He'd been deep in thought during breakfast and admitted under Charles's prodding that he thought he had a handle on something but needed time to work it out. He'd rushed through his meal and left abruptly. She had to be satisfied with the light touch he placed on her shoulder as an indication that she'd even been on his mind.

Or that he remembered the night before. They'd managed to create an oasis of their own in the shadows by the stairs leading to his room. Drunk under the power of his kisses, it had taken all the willpower she could dredge up not to ascend those stairs with him.

Santa Fe seemed almost deserted. The last exhibition had been given the night before, and most of the conclaves and tribes had packed up and left, as well as the swarms of tourists.

From Rosemary's satisfied expression, The Trading Post had topped previous records. "It will feel good to be just modestly busy after this past week." She smiled at her friend and employer. "You look like you have at least your toes back on earth. Maybe you should take another day off so you can fully join us poor humble mortals."

"You wouldn't act so smart if you didn't know I couldn't run this place without you," Charla returned with a wry smile. She glanced around the store, taking in the depleted stock. "And maybe I'll take you up on your suggestion. I should have brought my van so I could take a run to the pueblos and check our suppliers."

The door bell tinkled and Charla's eyes lighted when Jane Madrinez entered with John. The child ran up to her, displaying proudly the bandage on his finger.

"That one never sits still," Jane sighed, her ungainly body forcing her to move slowly. "He gets into everything. It will be good when school starts so he has something to use his energy." She unrolled the black cloth, exposing the turquoise and silver necklaces. "My brother is sorry about the loose fittings and hopes these meet with your approval."

They did, and Charla accepted them. "His pieces sold pretty well. Rosemary should have a nice check for you."

John remained behind as his aunt went to the office. "Miss Charla?" he asked hesitantly. "They said I shouldn't ask, but you did promise to take us on a picnic."

His face was so trusting and earnest. She had promised, but the days kept slipping away. Kirk had intimated that he was going to be busy, so perhaps today was a good time to take them.

"How does this afternoon sound?" she asked. "Do you think you can round up some of your friends?"

His black eyes grew round and shiny with happiness. "Oh, *yes!* I told them you wouldn't forget your promise!" he said proudly.

Her heart contracted. Had his friends been giving him a hard time, teasing him that the picnic would never materialize?

"I can take six in the van—and perhaps a teenager to help keep an eye on them," she suggested when she asked Jane if the picnic was agreeable with her.

She called Maria to prepare food for the picnic. Shortly after one, she was in the van and driving to the pueblo where she was certain John and his friends were waiting impatiently.

167

The sun was burning the landscape when she arrived, and she was having second thoughts about the outing. The snow- and rain-fed streams were dry this late in the summer, which made a cooling swim a lost hope, but she questioned the woman anyway.

Jane admitted not knowing of a creek that still held water. Debbie, a thin, reserved fifteen-year-old and sister to two of the boys, accompanied her. She proved exceptionally adept in keeping the high spirits of the little ones under control. It wasn't until they were on the road again that Debbie mentioned shyly that her brother had seen a water hole, all that remained of the creek running through Sinking Canyon. But that had been two weeks earlier. The inference was clear. Under the hot sun, it could have dried up by now.

Charla knew the place and decided it rated a chance. The steep sides of the canyon traveled in a north-south direction, so with luck, there should at least be some shade.

A half hour later she was maneuvering the van over the dry creek bed. At least one of her surmises was correct. The south wall was in shadow, and as Kirk had pointed out when they enjoyed the breeze under the arch, it was likely that any section protected from the unrelenting sun would in contrast be cool enough to create its own minicirculation.

John, sitting importantly in the seat beside her, was the first to see the water. With a yelp of joy, he soon had the others crowding forward to peer at the small pond.

Charla managed to bring the van close so they wouldn't have far to carry the food. Maria, bless her heart, had gone overboard and had filled the hamper and a box to overflowing.

The children fell out of the van and only her stern warning made them wait until she removed her sandals so she could check the depth of the water and look for hidden potholes. At no point did it rise over her knees, and with a whoop, the children raced into the water. They didn't own bathing suits, but she did manage to get them to remove their shirts and shoes first.

They had a marvelous time. Two hours later when Charla managed to get them out to eat, the pond was reduced to a huge mud puddle. But the children were blissfully happy and beamed through the layers of silt that had collected on them. She hoped their parents would be forgiving.

They fell on the food like locusts, leaving few crumbs behind. She managed to convince them to stay out of the pool and let the sun dry and warm them. Used to making up games with what was on hand, they were soon playing happily. They knew the terrain, and she had no qualms that they'd unknowingly stumble over a snake or tarantula.

Debbie proved to be a jewel, arbitrating arguments and preventing the more adventurous from wandering too far afield. She rescued one bent on reaching a shelf extending from the cliff high over their heads. Debbie's supervision of the children permitted Charla to relax and let her mind wander, to luxuriate in the wonder of Kirk and the exquisite sensations he so easily brought to life.

For the first time, she dared envision that there could be a future for them. In the beginning she'd gone no further than limiting the time frame that they had to his vacation. But surely he wasn't planning to disappear back to St. Louis after experiencing what they had shared! The possibility was like a cold hand on her heart, and she was glad when Debbie brought her from her suddenly depressing thoughts.

"They're pretty hot from playing, Miss Charla," she said shyly. "They've been good and want to know if they can go in the pond one more time."

The children stood clustered around the girl, their eyes bright with anticipation. She had enjoyed the water as much as her charges, and Charla couldn't deny them. Water was a precious commodity. There were so few places that they could play freely like this. So what if the inside of the van would get covered with mud? It needed a thorough cleaning anyway.

She noticed for the first time that the arroyo was filling with shade. The pool was in shadow, but the air was still warm. Looking up, she spotted a few dark clouds far off in the distance. From experience, she knew they were too far away to worry about. Any rain they might drop would bring no relief here.

"All right," she agreed indulgently. "It's getting late, but I don't think your parents will notice if you're wearing an additional layer of dirt."

With cries of delight, they stampeded down the slight incline to laugh uproariously as they flopped into the water. She went to the van and brought back several old sheets she used to pack around the pottery she picked up. They'd do well enough as towels. She then returned to the blanket and propped herself against a rock. A smile played on her lips as she watched the happy group splashing in their games. Slowly, part of her drifted away to be captured with memories of another time spent on a blanket, of looking up at the lovely natural arch swooping over her as kisses and long persuasive fingers brought her repeatedly to ecstasy . . .

"Miss Charla, I'm cold."

Charla snapped from her dream world to find a small shivering boy standing in front of her. The narrow canyon was almost completely in shadow. She gasped, appalled, when a glance at her watch revealed the late hour. It was almost six o'clock! What in the world was she doing, letting time slip away like that and forgetting her charges?

"Debbie, get everyone out immediately," she called. Why was she having this feeling of panic?

She rubbed the child briskly and ordered the others to do the same. There was a scramble to sort out shirts and shoes. Hurry, hurry, she wanted to scream. Tired after the day's activity, the children seemed to sense her dismay and became fretful. It seemed to take forever to get them into their clothes and assist with knotted shoelaces.

She didn't know when the sound started, only conscious that at some fringe of awareness she'd been hearing it for a while. It was a low rumble, almost like far-off thunder but not quite. Muffled by the high canyon walls, it was difficult to identify.

Debbie's head snapped up, and like an animal scenting danger, she stared north to where the sound was building beyond the twisting canyon. She was like a doe, ready for flight when she looked back at Charla. Her eyes held fright, and at that moment, Charla realized the cause of her own incipient panic. Those dark clouds had dumped their rain somewhere to the north. The drain-off of the rain had funneled into the canyon and at that very moment was racing toward them with the fury of a burst dam.

Her first thought was to get everyone in the van, but she'd once witnessed the tremendous speed with which the water traveled. She'd never get the van turned around and over the streambed in time.

The children were suddenly quiet, the sound having reached through their small talk. Living close to nature, they were able to sense danger, and they looked to her for direction.

"Climb, *quickly,*" she urged, fighting the debilitating panic tearing at her. They were at the bottom of the arroyo, and their only salvation lay in getting above the height of the water. And its height depended upon how much rain those clouds had dropped.

The children needed no second command. They scrambled up the steep side as surefootedly as wild goats. She followed them up the slope, steadying a slipping foot and ignoring the rain of stones loosened by those above her.

"The ledge," she gasped, giving them direction. It had looked sturdy enough when viewed from the bottom. Would it be strong enough to hold them all? From there

171

the side of the canyon rose steeply. She doubted any of them could climb higher. Please, Lord, let them all make it there safely, she prayed.

The roar was now shattering, reverberating between the canyon walls. It was impossible to even hear the stones rattle down past her. She spared a glance upward and saw that Debbie had reached the ledge and was assisting the youngsters up over the last obstacles.

Hesitantly, she looked down and was horrified to see that the streambed was flooding and the water was already washing over the hubcaps of the van. She pressed against the wall, dizzy from the knowledge of what would be happening to them if they'd taken that course of escape.

"Come this way, Miss Charla." Debbie's anxious call broke into her momentary palsy. "You're almost safe."

The remaining feet took the last of her energy. She had never been a mountain climber, and her fingers and knees were rubbed raw. She lay sprawled on the ledge, gulping in reviving oxygen before attempting to raise her head. A prayer of thanks escaped when she saw that the children were all accounted for.

With an explosive grinding roar, the wall of water tore around the last bend. It was at least fifteen feet high, and to her horror, she saw the van lifted effortlessly and tumbled like a toy as it was carried along on the crest of the rushing water.

The earsplitting noise seemed to go on forever, and when the raging crest swept on, Charla thought for a moment that she'd become deaf. It was the muffled cries of the youngest boy that brought her attention back to her charges. She gathered him close, murmuring soothingly until he grew quiet. The others were too shaken by what they'd witnessed to do more than look dumbly at the holocaust below them. Then one by one they turned to her. She was the adult. She would get them safely out of this.

Their trust shook her. The abrasions on her hands and legs burned, and for a shaken moment, her eyes burned with suppressed tears. She peered carefully over the ledge. The muddy water was still rushing by, and she knew it could continue for some time. That way of escape was closed. She looked up, hoping for some path, some hint of irregularity, but the wall rose without a toehold in sight.

Their precarious position hit her then, causing a moment of panic. They were stuck there for the night unless they were found before dusk. Then the awful truth crashed down on her. No one would know where to search for them. No one knew where they were. The frightening possibility was that they'd be stuck there until morning. By then the water would be down to a trickle, and they could climb down and make their way out.

It was going to be a long, cold night, and she prayed that they wouldn't catch pneumonia. The children's pants were still damp, and she was dressed in a thin shirt and shorts. The canyon was already in deep shadow, giving up its heat. Luckily, the stone walls would retain it longer. If she kept them huddled together, they might be able to make it without too much trauma.

"It looks like we'll be roughing it for the night, pardners," she said bracingly to their upturned faces.

CHAPTER EIGHTEEN

When Kirk woke up that morning, there was no doubt in his mind what had to be done. He had to get this case finished and off his mind so nothing interfered with wooing Charla. There was going to be no more frustration from having to end an evening with a kiss and go to bed tied up in knots. He'd found the woman he wanted to spend the rest of his life with. His only problem was getting her to admit that she felt the same way. From her responses, he didn't think it would be difficult, but he was too unsure in this game of love to take anything for granted.

His instinct was telling him that he already had the pieces to the puzzle of what was happening at Treemont and only needed to get them into some semblance of order so they made sense. His plan was to go to the plant and follow through the various processes from the raw material to the finished product and on to the end where it was packaged for shipment. Somewhere during the process, someone—was there more than one person involved?—was able to cabbage rejected products and slip them through the stringent quality controls that were set up at various checkpoints.

He arrived early at the plant, and as he locked the car, he was greeted guardedly by several other workers arriving at the same time. They looked at the Jaguar with covetous eyes. Larry Perkins joined the group, and the usual questions came about performance on the road and gas mileage.

"I've an order in for one," Perkins announced. "I decided I might as well go for broke. A person only lives once."

The others nodded in agreement. They knew that the year before, his wife had taken off with another guy. A man needed something to bolster his self-esteem.

The parking lot was filling, and they all trooped in to their jobs. Soon the machines were running at full capacity, filling the air with a muted hum. With controlled patience Kirk followed the various procedures, questioning when necessary but mostly observing. By lunchtime he was beginning to doubt his reasoning.

He'd had a hearty breakfast and wasn't hungry, but he decided a cup of coffee would hit the spot. Disliking the coffee from the automatic machines, he thought of the superlative brew that Perkins made. Perhaps the man could be coerced into sharing another cup.

His office was empty, as was his coffee maker, and Kirk turned away in disgust. He spied Pete, who had pulled a chair up at the end of the packing table and was eating a thick-sliced sandwich for his lunch. Kirk hadn't expected the new father to show up, and he went to him to ask how the baby and mother were doing.

"He's a hungry one," Pete said proudly. "He keeps his mother drained dry." The restraint he'd felt before with this tall man was gone. They'd shared an intimate event together, and a tenuous bond had been created.

"He looks like he'll be football material when he grows up," Kirk teased, recalling the chubby cheeks, the healthy indignant cry for attention.

Pete looked at him oddly. "That's what old Matia said. She saw him going to college and running with a football."

So Matia foretold the future as well as delivered babies. Kirk remembered from his childhood how the older Indians believed in such predictions. He wondered what she would make of this problem he was wrestling with.

"I was hoping to get a decent cup of coffee from Perkins. Do you know where he is?"

Kirk was surprised by the man's instant withdrawal. Pete put his sandwich down and stared at it for a long minute before he spoke. "Sally made me promise to speak to you," he said through set lips. "I was not drunk the other day. I found out early that it didn't agree with me, and I do not touch alcohol."

Kirk looked at the man, feeling embarrassed. Kirk had come down unnecessarily hard on him, but why deny the obvious?

Pete's dark eyes grew hard when he saw Kirk's disbelief. "Think back, Mr. Webster. You evidently found a bottle next to me, but did you smell any wine on me? That's what Sally noticed, and when I came out of the daze I was in, we did a lot of talking."

Kirk thought back, recalling his disgust and anger when coming upon Pete huddled in the nest of packing crates. Had there been any odor of alcohol? It should have been there if Pete had drunk enough to make him pass out. He hated the thought that he'd jumped to an unjust conclusion just because of circumstantial evidence.

"What are you inferring?" he asked, his senses alert.

Pete's eyes dodged around the room before resting on him. "We decided that I was drugged."

Kirk stared at him while absorbing all the implications raised by that statement. "How?"

"The last thing I can recall clearly was joining Perkins for our usual coffee break."

Kirk's alarm system went into high gear. "Why would he want to drug you?" Pete was laying it on the line. There was no reason to pretend he didn't understand what he was inferring.

"That's what we tried to understand. Then yesterday when you asked him about the banged-up boxes, it all made sense. One thing I know for certain is that no box that I handle gets so much as a mark on it." The assertion was said with pride. "I was desperate for work when Miss Charla got me this job. It made it possible for us to start building our home. It didn't take Sally to remind me that we owe Miss Charla for all that we have."

"What are you telling me?"

"That Perkins needed me out of the way so he could mark up some boxes. And he needed them in a hurry." Dark eyes challenged Kirk to believe him.

It all fell together neatly with what he was suspecting, Kirk realized. Now all he needed was to get the proof. It was time to call Charles and get him in on this. The next step would require the power of his position.

In the end, it wasn't that difficult. Perkins hadn't the hardened background of a criminal. He came to Charles's office already frightened. Backed into a corner with Kirk's questioning and Charles's demanding presence, Perkins folded.

He'd been approached by a rival company who had missed out on the government bid and sorely wanted it. The plan had seemed foolproof, the extra money enticing. He made a practice of showing up at the plant proper and making friends with the inspectors. He was frequently on hand when a part was rejected. When possible he'd make off with it and exchange it for one on the shelf ready for shipment. There had been no trouble requisitioning spare boxes to seal them in. It had been done quickly when Pete was off with his forklift. It was then easy enough to substitute it for a box he'd already purposely damaged.

The day he had resorted to dropping the drug in Pete's coffee, no order had come to send Pete to the plant for a pickup. He had two defective parts all wrapped and ready to be placed on the shelves. The rumors were out for the reason behind Kirk's endless questioning with his eagle eyes. Perkins had been scared that the defective parts might be found in his possession. He waited until Pete stumbled, drugged, into the corner where the empty crates were kept. In an inspired moment, he'd tossed the half-empty bottle next to him and made the switch. He heard Kirk approaching just in time to escape out the loading door. He waited there, smoking several cigarettes to calm his shattered nerves over the close call he'd had.

Dusk was falling when Kirk got back to the hacienda. Charles pulled in behind him, and they walked to the house together, discussing the options opened to them now that the mystery was solved.

Maria accosted them at the door, her face creased with worry. "Charla isn't back. She said she'd have the children out for just a few hours and would be back here by six."

In between her frequent cries of concern, they managed to get the story from her. She'd packed a large picnic lunch, and Charla had picked up some children to take them on a long-promised outing.

"I see nothing to worry about," Charles said soothingly. "They were no doubt having such a good time that they stayed longer than planned. You know how Charla is with children."

"Perhaps she's having trouble with the van," Kirk suggested worriedly. A tension was tightening his muscles, and he wondered if he were just feeding off Maria's concern.

"If that's the case, the roads are heavily traveled now what with everyone's going home," Charles informed him. "The Indians all know her. She'd have no problem getting help."

But what if it happened at some out-of-the-way spot? Kirk wanted to protest. The phone rang and Charles went to answer it. He returned minutes later, his face pale under its tan.

"That was the police on the reservation. Some of the parents contacted them. The children haven't returned. It seems there was a heavy rainstorm back in the mountains.

178

Several of the creeks are already flooding from the drain-off. They don't know if the picnic was in any of the canyons and wondered if we had any idea where they can start looking."

Maria gave a high trembling wail. "I knew, I knew. Oh, my poor baby!"

Kirk paled as his insides twisted. They all knew stories about how the water poured down from the mountains unable to absorb the flood, changing the dry arroyos into raging torrents and sweeping everything before it. Not his Charla! He was blinded from the horror of that possibility.

Charles and Kirk paused long enough to get the name of the pueblo from Maria, and the two ran from the house. Kirk swore violently when he saw that the Lincoln blocked his Jaguar. Charles placed the key in the outstretched hand. This was no time for arguments. Kirk was the more experienced driver, and the Lincoln was fast enough.

All records were broken. They pulled in front of the general store with a squeal of tires. A police car was in front, and from the people gathered there, it was evident this was the command post.

The policeman had little new to add. There were six children all under ten and a fifteen-year-old girl, sister of two of the boys. All the men in the area were mobilized and out looking, and for the first time, Kirk noticed that there were only women in the store with unnaturally silent children clinging to their skirts.

"If only we had some idea in which direction they went, we could concentrate there," the officer said tiredly. "There's nothing you can do," he added when Kirk's restlessness demanded an outlet. "You don't know the terrain here, and a flashlight won't help you much. You'll end up lost and we'll have to waste time finding you. The men out there know where to look. I suggest you go home. We'll call you as soon as we hear anything."

Kirk's burning look stopped the officer from making further idiotic suggestions. The man shrugged his shoulders and turned to his two-way radio when it squawked.

It was the longest night Kirk had ever put in. Some of the women gathered the children and took them home. The others sat quietly in a corner, checking that the coffee-pot was filled and the sandwiches replaced. Later, when the night air got cold, they produced a pot of hot soup.

The men drifted in sporadically to check if anything had turned up. They drank the coffee and ate the soup before returning wearily to comb the dead-end canyons and the arroyos that cut through the rocky land.

At three in the morning the first break came. A van was found twisted almost out of recognition. Could they come to positively identify it? Kirk's heart stopped for a second, and he knew what it was like to die until the voice continued from a hazy distance that, no, no bodies were found in it.

They followed the battered truck for a mile off the high-way. Charles was immune when his car occasionally bottomed in the ruts. They picked up a swollen stream, the waters black with silt and debris. The truck finally halted, and their joint headlights outlined the van lying on its side with the water swirling around it. The two men stepped out of the car, their bodies heavy with dread. The logo for The Trading Post could be seen clearly on the door.

It had been dropped near the edge of the stream, and they waded knee-deep to peer into it. Kirk rested his head against the muddy frame as waves of relief swept over him. The van was empty. He could still hope.

"Is that where it came from?" he asked. The sky was lined with stars. Under the pale light, the water poured from the narrow canyon, but the steep walls kept it in stygian darkness.

The man nodded silently. His nephew was one of the missing children.

Kirk took an impatient step forward. "Then what are we doing standing here? Let's get going."

"I tried it. The water is up to my shoulders. The land dips and it gets deeper once you get in the canyon." He'd fortunately had a dry change of clothes stuffed behind his seat. The soggy clothes in the back of his truck gave mute evidence of how the swift waters had swept him off his feet during his attempt.

"But we can't just stand here and do nothing!" Kirk shouted in frustration.

The man looked at him sadly. "In the morning the water will be down enough so we should be able to get in. We will also be able to see."

Kirk wanted to rage at such fatalistic acceptance. Didn't the man understand that his Charla was trapped somewhere in that demon canyon, perhaps hurt and needing him?

"I'll go back and tell them," the man said quietly. "We'll come back as soon as there's enough light to see."

"Why don't you go with him and get some rest?" Kirk urged Charles, aware for the first time how haggard he looked.

"I'll wait with you," Charles said firmly. "Let's try for some sleep in the car."

They crawled into the car and turned off the lights. They had enough of the grisly sight of the overturned van. Exhausted, Kirk leaned against the seat and closed his eyes as the pain washed over him. How could he face an existence without Charla in his life? Images flashed in an unceasing progression through his mind. Charla, her head thrown back as she gave her chuckling laugh . . . Charla looking dreamily at him, her incredible eyes dark with passion . . . He could feel her lips softened under his, taste the wonder of her that waited there. His eyes squeezed tight in a desperate need to banish the torture the pictures triggered.

He never told her he loved her! The despair of that omission tore at him. How could he survive knowing he would never hold her in his arms again? He pulled in a deep

181

breath. He had to believe in miracles. It was the only way he could make it through the night.

Kirk awoke with a jerk. He stared bleary-eyed at the sky lighted with the first faint predawn blush. His head swiveled to check the stream. The Indian had been right. Even in the faint light, he could see that the water had receded to a faint trickle, leaving a scattering of pools between muddy stretches.

He glanced at the backseat. Charles had managed to find a position he could sleep in. One look at the man's exhausted face, and he let himself quietly out of the car. He would go first. It would be better if he saved the older man from the worst.

The mud sucked at his shoes, slowing his progress, until in exasperation he stepped out of them. He gave up counting the number of times he slipped on the slick mud or forced his way through clumps of tree branches and climbed over heaps of gravel that shifted treacherously under foot.

The first time he heard the voices, he dismissed the sounds as his overeager imagination. He'd just gotten over the shock of digging a cloth out of the mud, afraid to find what was attached to it. It had been just that, and he was still reeling from his relief.

He rounded a bend and stood in disbelief when he saw a tall thin girl urging on several incredibly filthy boys as they trudged wearily toward him. Fifty feet beyond them was a woman, her thick plait of hair half undone and every part of her smeared with mud. She was carrying a whimpering child and was picking her way carefully around the endless obstacles.

He never saw anyone look more beautiful.

All the pent-up worry, the desperate night spent in fear rose up to erupt in an uncontrollable explosion.

"You've done it again, brat!" he roared. "Of all the stupid pranks you've pulled, this has to take the prize!"

Their mouths dropped open in shocked surprise. The

small boy wriggled from Charla's arms and ran to his sister.

"You're almost out of here, kids," he said, lowering his voice with effort. "I daresay your families will be waiting for you by the time you get there."

They needed no further urging. They were off with renewed energy, and Kirk turned to the woman waiting for him with wide stunned eyes.

He had no recall of eliminating the distance. She was in his arms and his mouth was hungrily kissing hers. Not until he was certain that he wasn't fantasizing again did he ease the pressure.

"I'm not going through this again," he vowed when he caught his breath. "I'm not having you wander around the countryside without having any idea where you are. You're going to marry me, do you hear me?"

Her blue eyes were red-rimmed and incredibly beautiful as they glared at him. "Is that a proposal, Kirk Webster? If it is, you know what you can do with it!" She had spent a sleepless night using all her energy to retain her control. Exhaustion had brought sleep to the children, but she'd lived in horror that one might move in their sleep and roll off the ledge. It was Kirk and memories of their hours together that had helped her keep her sanity. And the promise that once out of the hellish situation she had something important to tell him. But now, with him yelling at her like a demented man, she'd be damned if she'd tell him she loved him.

A smile tugged on his lips as his voice gentled. "And you'd be only too happy to assist, wouldn't you? I'm doing it all wrong, aren't I? But if you knew the hell I've been living through ever since we found your van . . ."

Her expression softened, realizing what he must have been experiencing not knowing what happened to them or if they were even alive.

"Would it help if I got on my knees and started all over?

I love you, sweet Charla. Will you marry me, be my wife, and have my babies?"

Joy raced through her, banishing the terrible weariness. "Get up out of the mud, you fool," she laughed through her tears. "How can I kiss you when you're down there?"

EPILOGUE

Under the enormous pink-and-white-striped tent, the string quartet began the "Wedding March," and the guests rose in unison. Kirk, with his father beside him as best man, also turned. He gritted his teeth in annoyance when he realized his view down the aisle was obstructed. He smiled slightly when John and a small blond girl walked toward him, their eyes large with the responsibility of remembering their instructions. Debbie followed with carefully measured steps, her thin face aglow with the wonder of being in this procession. A finger surreptitiously touched the material of the pink dress. She'd never worn anything so spectacular. Behind her came Rosemary in a deeper rose dress, and then Kirk tensed, hearing the gasps of pleasure.

He saw Charles first, tall and proud as he glanced down at his daughter on his arm. Then she was there and Kirk's throat tightened. He had thought Charla beautiful in spite of the mud and bruises when he saw she was safe that agonizing time two weeks before. Now she was breathtakingly gorgeous. She was wearing her mother's wedding gown of ivory lace. Her hair hung free to her waist, as he loved it, and he knew she had left it so just for him. In her hands was a cascade of pink and white roses. The flowers were repeated in a coronet around her head.

As if feeling the compelling force of his gaze, her eyes

185

rose and met his. *I love you.* The vow was exchanged with burning intensity as she moved slowly to his side.

"I think we're to be congratulated," Tyson said happily hours later as the party tossed paper rose petals at the departing couple. The vows had been exchanged, the toasts had been given as the champagne flowed, and the catered meal had been superb.

Charles nodded, beaming over their success. "Someday when they come down off their cloud I hope they'll appreciate all the work we put into this wedding."

"I thought they were crazy insisting they wanted to be married in two weeks. At least we talked them out of having it done by a justice of the peace. It's lucky we had already done that preliminary checking and could pull this together."

They had reason to be pleased. Their war plan had succeeded beyond their wildest expectations.

"It's a good thing I didn't make any reservations at those places we came up with for their honeymoon." Charles had felt disgruntled when Kirk had dismissed all their suggestions and had kept secret what plans he'd made.

Tyson looked at his old friend with concern. "You're accepting Charla's move to St. Louis?" She had put Rosemary in charge of The Trading Post and had talked about opening a branch in that city.

"It might not be for long," Charles said hopefully. "Last night at the stag party you gave Kirk, he mentioned the possibility of moving his office here to Albuquerque. You'd have them near you, and it's only a short drive from Santa Fe."

Tyson's face lighted with pleasure. "Think of the fun we'll have baby-sitting the grandchildren!"

Charles pulled the slightly battered white notepad from his pocket and flipped it to the last page. "That reminds me, what do you think of 'Tracy' as a name for one of the girls?"

Tyson savored it on his tongue and nodded. "Not bad. And how about 'Jason' for the next son?" He watched as the names were added to the list. He noticed it had grown to six. Well, why not?

The pad was put away, and the two men exchanged grins wide with shared delight over a job well done. They turned back to the tent with arms placed companionably across each other's shoulders.

There were two hundred guests waiting, give or take a dozen. Now the party could get on in earnest.